"I won't   won't
be watche   d.

"Solve the   y with me."
"Do you al   tly as you please?"
"Always." He picked up the nightgown of pale silk she'd laid out on the bed and put his face to it, inhaling its scent. "You smell like flowers at dawn that are just beginning to open their petals to the sensual warmth of the day."

Sydney felt her legs go weak, and tried to hide a shiver of awareness. "How would you know what flowers smell like at dawn? You only come out at night, like some kind of vampire."

He laughed warmly, fully. Then he crossed to where she stood and wrapped the nightgown around her neck to pull her to him. "I like the night, Sydney. Maybe you are right, and I am a vampire. Maybe I need to drink from your innocence and your passion to live." His next words were a whisper. "If you find that is the truth, what will you do? Will you run?"

Silk . . . silk around her neck . . . words spoken with the sensuality of silk . . . his breath soft as silk on her mouth. It was too much. . . .

WHAT ARE *LOVESWEPT* ROMANCES?

They are stories of true romance and touching emotion. We believe those two very important ingredients are constants in our highly sensual and very believable stories in the *LOVESWEPT* line. Our goal is to give you, the reader, stories of consistently high quality that may sometimes make you laugh, sometimes make you cry, but are always fresh and creative and contain many delightful surprises within their pages.

Most romance fans read an enormous number of books. Those they truly love, they keep. Others may be traded with friends and soon forgotten. We hope that each *LOVESWEPT* romance will be a treasure—a "keeper." We will always try to publish

LOVE STORIES YOU'LL NEVER FORGET
BY AUTHORS YOU'LL ALWAYS REMEMBER

The Editors

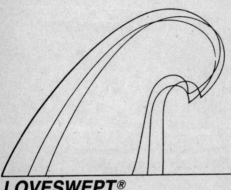

LOVESWEPT®

Fayrene Preston

The Delaneys of Killaroo: Sydney, The Temptress

BANTAM BOOKS
TORONTO • NEW YORK • LONDON • SYDNEY • AUCKLAND

THE DELANEYS OF KILLAROO: SYDNEY, THE TEMPTRESS

A Bantam Book / September 1987

ISBN 0-553-21874-3

Published simultaneously in the United States and Canada

Bantam Books are published by Bantam Books, Inc. Its trademark, consisting of the words "Bantam Books" and the por-
trayal of a rooster, is Registered in U.S. Patent and Trademark
Office and in other countries. Marca Registrada. Bantam
Books, Inc., 666 Fifth Avenue, New York, New York 10103.

PRINTED IN THE UNITED STATES OF AMERICA

O   0 9 8 7 6 5 4 3 2 1

To my agent, Denise Marcil, for all the hard and dedicated work required for the Delaney projects, for always being there for me, for caring, thank you.

And to Kay Hooper and Iris Johansen, for the friendship, for the support and understanding, for the fun!

About the Delaney Dynasty . . .

When William Delaney was born in 1855, men were men and the West was wild. There were Indian troubles for settlers, but not for the Delaneys; old Shamus had cannily invested one of his sons in a marriage to the daughter of an Apache chief a year or so before young William's birth, which quieted things considerably.

Of course, William, like his uncles before him, gleefully borrowed the Indian custom of counting "coup" and on occasion rode pell-mell through peaceful Apache camps screeching madly and attempting to touch as many braves as possible before they angrily chased him back to Killara, the Delaney homestead.

If he had run true to form, old Shamus, never one to spare the rod, would have punished his grandson severely, but he didn't. He'd learned it was useless in dealing with William. Trees were scarce in southern Arizona, and more than one eastern-made paddle had been worn out on William's unrepentant bottom.

William's father, Desmond, second of Shamus's nine sons, was killed in the Civil War in 1862, leaving seven-year-old William in the care of his mother, Anne, his grandparents, and various uncles, aunts, and cousins. If he had lived, perhaps Desmond would have controlled his son, for the boy had worshipped him.

Of those left to guard him, only his grandfather had any sort of control over the boy, and that was little enough. Old Shamus, loving his grandchildren as he had his sons, certainly tried. Since William possessed the Delaney charm and was smart enough to turn it to good effect, even Shamus found himself easing up on the boy and remarking that his misdemeanors were products of high spirits.

The Apaches, understandably annoyed, disagreed; good Irish whiskey was called for then to ease the pain of lacerated temper.

But as William grew, it began to require more than a friendly drink to repair the consequences of his reckless actions. William rode wild horses, searched far and wide for wild women, and discovered both cards and drink a good ten years before he should have.

At the age of sixteen William had perfected the rather dangerous art of escaping out bedroom windows, enraged husbands and loaded guns one step behind him. He had, with forethought, trained his savage mustang to stand just so beneath those windows, and husbands in jealous pursuit found themselves choking on dust and listening to hearty laughter carried away by fleet hooves.

By the time he was eighteen William had searched

out and conquered women within a two-hundred-mile radius of Killara. Indeed, betting in saloons held that a pair of his boots could be found under the bed of every woman under thirty except those William was kin to.

And since old Shamus was no fool, he was well aware of why his grandson often arrived home sketchily attired in only his trousers. Shamus could forgive the womanizing, merely remarking somewhat irritably that he could have raised all nine of his sons and shod them handsomely in the boots William had left behind him.

However, men *were* men then, and the West was still somewhat wild. And, inevitably, William was a bit lazy in leaving a warm bed one night. The jealous husband had burst in prepared, gun in hand and temper raging. William wasted no time with his pants, but grabbed his own gun instead, and when he left that window there was a badly wounded man behind him.

William might have stood his trial; he might even have been acquitted. But he was a gambler, and he knew the odds: at least half the men on any jury would be men he had wronged. So he climbed aboard his bad-tempered mustang and headed west.

He took with him little in the way of material things, confident of his luck, but he did "borrow" a single treasure from the Delaney family coffers. As treasures go, the necklace was worth little. It consisted of three silver medallions, each bearing a turquoise stone. Perhaps William was thinking of his grandfather's lucky number; in any event, he took the necklace.

On the Barbary Coast he found men even more dangerous than those he had left behind him; though there were warm beds aplenty, there were also eager guns and short tempers. William, ever ready to conquer virgin territory, cocked his eye still farther west and boarded a ship.

He wound up, somewhat to his own surprise, in Australia, and liked it enough to remain for a while. He worked when he had to and gambled when he could, arriving at last on a sheep station—where he hired on happily after a glance at the boss's very pretty daughter.

It was in 1877 when William went to work there, and he lost no time in leaving yet another pair of boots under yet another bed. But William had reckoned without Matthew Devlin, the quiet man whose only child was his daughter, Mary. William went to his wedding as lighthearted as always, unperturbed by the shotgun that guided his steps to the altar.

William remained for a short time, long enough to tell his bride all about his family in Arizona, about Killara. Truly of Shamus's blood, he wove a splendid story about the relatives half a world away, gifting them with even more wealth and power than what was actually theirs at the time. Then, being William, he cheerfully abandoned his bride and sailed for home, trusting of forgiveness behind him, welcome before him, and having no idea that he had left in Australia something more than a pair of boots and an old necklace.

William found, at Killara, that there was indeed welcome, and that past misdeeds, if not forgotten, were at least viewed as dim and unimportant. He returned to the bosom of his family and never thought to mention the small matter of a wife left behind in Australia's outback.

Unfortunately, none of William's adventures had taught him to curb his recklessness, and he lost no time in reminding people of why he had left Arizona years before. He went his charming way from bad to worse, until even his loving grandfather freely predicted that he would end by getting his neck stretched.

Which, regrettably, is exactly how things turned out.

Mary Delaney was not surprised by William's abandonment; she had loved him and, perhaps remarkably, understood him. She would have as soon attempted to chain the wind as tie William to her side. And she was a strong woman, a proud woman. So she bore her son, Charles, and raised him on the station alone after her father died. She told him often the story of Killara and the Arizona Delaneys, that and a necklace being the only birthright William had left his son.

In his turn, Charles married and fathered a son, passing on the tales of Killara—which was, in reality, by that time, all that William had described and more.

As with many families, the Australian branch of the Delaney clan could boast at least one mystery, and William's son, Charles, was responsible for theirs. At some point in his young life, he attempted to mine gems, and having barely fathered his own son, he was murdered because of a fabulous gem it was believed he had found. His killers were never caught and the gem, if it existed, vanished.

By the time Spencer Delaney, William's great-grandson, was born in 1935, Killara had become a legend; with news spreading worldwide overnight because of advanced technology, hard facts upheld the legend.

And, pride being a strong Delaney trait, Spencer did not turn to his wealthy American relations when he found himself in financial trouble. Instead, he sold off the larger part of the station to a neighboring station, requiring only that his family be given a two-month option to repurchase the land if it came up for resale.

Killaroo, as the station had been renamed by Mary, was small, and the sale of the land was only temporarily helpful to the family. Spencer, realizing too late what he had given up, worked his fingers to the bone to see his family prosper so the land could be restored to them. As the years passed, it became his obsession. He suffered two minor heart attacks and, ignoring warnings by his doctor that a third would be likely to kill him, continued to work and scheme to get his land back.

Since Delaneys tended to sire male children, it was somewhat surprising that Spencer had fathered three girls. And though Spencer may well have felt the lack of a son, he loved his girls and wanted the best for them. Sydney, Matilda, and Adelaide, however, wanted their father healthy and free from worry.

And so, when the land once belonging to them came up for sale, the girls resolved to raise the staggering price. They knew, of course, of their American cousins, but none of them even suggested that those strangers be applied to.

Each had a scheme. Each had a talent, or a means to make money quickly. And each was driven, as never before in her life, to attain a very specific goal. They were fighting for their birthright, but, even more, they were fighting for their father's life.

They had two months. Sixty days to do the impossible. And if they knew it *was* impossible, the knowledge was unimportant to them. They were Delaneys, and it was bred into them to know that even the impossible road was traveled one step at a time.

And so they began.

Prologue

Her father would never agree to her plan if he knew, Sydney thought as she watched him through the kitchen window. Excessive gambling right after her mother had died had lost him the large portion of the Killaroo land he was now striving so desperately to earn back.

But short of embezzling from the bank where she worked, gambling was the only plan she could come up with. It was a wild, perhaps even dangerous scheme, but it could work. She had a fine mind, with a penchant for mathematics, and if she had never actually gambled herself, she could certainly learn, she told herself.

She and her sisters were sitting at the kitchen table of the place that had been her home all her life, the homestead of her family's sheep station in New South Wales. The kitchen of Killaroo was a place of warmth and happy memories. She could still remember her mother, so loving and beautiful, busy at the stove. It was a place where family crises, big or small, were worked out. Now they had gathered for the biggest crisis they had ever faced.

Her eyes were drawn back to the window and her father beyond, bent over the old tractor, trying to fix it one more time.

Illness and age had diminished his once tall, lanky frame, and suffering had marked his craggy face. Over the past twenty-six years of her life, there had been countless times when she had run to him with her problems. His strength had been her support. His gentleness had eased her tears. His advice and warm humor had gotten her over the toughest times, when the humiliation her stutter was causing her threatened to swamp her. If she was in any way a success today, it was because of him.

Now it was her turn to help him.

With renewed resolve, Sydney turned back to her two sisters. "So we're agreed?"

"Right. We've got to keep our individual goals in mind, but if one of us needs help, the others will come running," Manda said. "We've got to remember this is a joint project. We *all* must succeed."

Addie nodded in agreement. "But what about Dad? It's important to keep this a secret. There's potential danger in all our plans, and we can't worry him." She made a face. "You two have it a hell of a lot easier than I do. He's bound to hear what I'm doing."

"Do the best you can," Sydney said. "And if you need help, ring us."

"I'll be on the move, so I'll check in often," Addie

said. "And since I'll be closest to home, I'll keep an eye on Dad."

"Good," Sydney said. "Be sure and let us know if anything changes with him."

Manda drew a deep, shaky breath. "Lord, I'm scared. What if we blow it?"

"I'm scared too," Addie said softly.

Sydney couldn't stand the fact that her two younger sisters might be frightened—Addie, who looked so fragile but in reality was as strong as the sun that shone over Australia, and Manda, who viewed life as one long grand adventure. She reached for her sisters' hands and clasped each one tightly. "We all are," she said. "But we won't fail, because we can't." She smiled with an effort. "This isn't another one of Manda's trips to the sea. This dream has to become a reality."

As she held her sisters' hands, Sydney felt the warmth and strength flowing between the three of them. To an outsider, it might appear that the odds were against them. After all, one million five hundred thousand dollars was an enormous sum of money for three young women to earn in such a short period of time. But an outsider would be reckoning without their love of their father and for one another. They would succeed.

One

One floor above the casino, from behind the one-way glass, Nicholas Charron watched her, as he had every night for the past three nights.

Her name was Sydney Delaney. He had gotten this information from the registration card she had filled out when she had arrived on the island three days ago. Alone.

With each night that passed, his curiosity about her grew. She seemed intensely interested in the games, but she had yet to place a bet. And he had seen several men approach her, but with scarcely a look she had sent them on their way.

From his remote observation post he had a complete view of the entire casino. Men and women dressed in their evening finery milled below him in a rhythm of bright color and swirling motion, uncaring that just beyond the casino's wide expanse of windowed walls lay the wonder and the glory of the Great Barrier Reef. Their disregard of the natural beauty of the reef and the star-brilliant night above it amused him. While most casinos were windowless, his was not. He deliberately had had the windows included in the design as his own private joke—just as he had had giant sea-water aquariums set in the long wall that ran across the back of the casino. Although the aquariums featured the vividly patterned fish that swam in the waters of the reef, he knew that to the majority of the people in the casino, the fish provided little more than an exotic backdrop for the real reason they had come to the island—the gaming.

He understood people, their vices, their greed. Soon, Nicholas promised himself, he would understand Sydney Delaney.

He turned away from the window and walked to the long row of monitors that provided coverage of the entire casino. With a quick flick of a series of switches, four screens glowed simultaneously with her image.

Sydney Delaney was clearly beautiful, but there were many women in his casino tonight who were as beautiful, if not more so. Yet there was something about her that had drawn his attention to her and had kept it there. Unprecedented for him.

Once, a long time ago, he had seen a figurine of a young girl in a Chicago store window, so fine and delicate, she appeared translucent, so fragile and expensive, a glass dome had protected her. He had wanted the figurine. The woman below reminded him of that figurine.

He looked closer, trying to decipher, to take apart and thus explain, the pull she was exerting on him. Her hair seemed a dark burgundy and hung in a lustrous mass to her shoulders. He frowned, for the color seemed to contain a depth that the screen of the monitor couldn't satisfactorily register.

In the monitor that caught her profile he saw a straight nose and a clean sweep of jaw. Another monitor showed him finely shaped brows arched over wide, light-colored eyes of an undiscernable shade and a disconcerting mouth, full and perfectly formed to fit under a man's lips.

A third monitor revealed a full-length picture of her. The long dress she wore was of cream-colored slipper satin. The neckline was high, but the back dipped to the waist, exposing skin that, on the monitor at least, appeared flawless. In involuntary anticipation of the time when he would touch that flawless skin, his fingers curled, one by one, into his palm.

Experience told him that most of the gowns on the women in the casino revealed more and cost more than the one she wore, but it didn't matter. Any clothing would look marvelous on her, he concluded.

There was an elegance about her and a grace, even as she remained still, and motion and noise swirled around her—like the sea that surrounded the island . . . his island, the Isle of Charron.

Did she have that much command over her emotions and nerves? he wondered. The question intrigued him.

His mind returned briefly to the glass dome that had surrounded the fragile figurine years before. Glass could be broken.

• • • •

If a panther could live on a tropical island, his name would surely be Nicholas Charron, Sydney decided. She had never seen him, but she could *feel* him—like a violent disturbance in the atmosphere.

Strangely, she never questioned why she felt he was there above her, watching. She just did. She knew that he paced in his control room above the casino, and she sensed his eyes on her, like a warm breath across her skin.

The fact that he was observing her from behind a one-way mirror made her feel exposed, unprotected, and it was a feeling she hated above all else. But she dealt with the vulnerability he was opening up in her as she always did—with absolute control over her body and her mind.

As was her way, she never went into any situation blind if she could help it. Before she had come to the Isle of Charron, she had researched the island, the casino, and the man who owned both. She had learned a great deal, but not all.

Nicholas Charron was a mysterious man. It was known that he was an American expatriate, but exactly what he had done from the time he left America to the time he bought the Isle of Charron was shrouded in mystery. However, over the last five years he had developed an island resort and casino like nothing Australia had seen before, especially on the Great Barrier Reef. They called his casino and hotel complex Charron's Glass Palace—like everything else on the island, his name was attached, whether he intended it to be or not. As a result, the Isle of Charron had gained an international reputation among jet setters and high rollers. They came to spend money, to have a good time, and if possible to see Nicholas Charron.

Speculation ran high, and extraordinary things were whispered about him. He had an aura that was as dark as the night, and to the thrill-seeking gamblers, his mystique was as big a draw as his casino.

But he never came down onto the casino floor, and only rarely did he invite anyone to his suite at the top of the resort complex. Unless . . .

People talked and word spread. She hadn't been on the island more than a day, when an excited lady she had encountered on the beach had told her that sometimes Nicholas Charron would stand in his control room above the casino floor and scan the action below him to choose a woman for the night.

Sydney had watched women do things she knew were calculated to attract the attention of the dark man everyone talked about but very few ever saw. Somehow she had known the women wouldn't be successful. Somehow she had known it was *she* he watched.

She was being pursued by someone who couldn't be seen, only felt, but Sydney refused to give in to the agitation that ran through her veins with a singing excitement. She had to keep her mind on her purpose for being in the casino. Since she had been on the island, she had carefully studied the action of each of the games, and to-night she had chosen craps to observe. It was a fast-paced game, and the chances of winning large amounts of money seemed good. Wondering about the odds, she opened her purse and pulled out a small calculator.

Within the space of a few seconds two men stood on either side of her.

And watching from the control room, Nicholas Charron reached for the phone.

One man was big and muscular and had a face so grooved and pitted, it looked as if it had been pulled straight off the side of Ayers Rock. The other man, an Oriental, was short and wiry with flat black eyes that stared at her without expression.

It was the larger of the two men who spoke. "I'm sorry, miss, you'll have to come with us."

There was something inherently threatening about these two men that caught Sydney totally off guard, and her heart constricted in fright too quickly for her to suppress it. "B-b-but why?"

"You'll have to come with us to the security office. No one is allowed to use a calculator in the casino."

Sydney was furious with herself. It was the first time in a long while she had stuttered in front of a stranger, and it was her own fault. If she hadn't been so absorbed in thought about the mysterious owner of the casino, she would have seen these men coming toward her and prepared herself to confront them.

She waited until she was sure she had her nerves under control, and she would be able to speak calmly. "I'm sorry. I didn't realize. I'll put it away."

The man's hand closed on her elbow as he prepared to urge her forward. "Come with me, please."

A courteous man, she thought. A dangerous man. She wasn't going anywhere with him.

"Excuse me, Miss Delaney?"

She whirled to find yet another man. This one was tall and good-looking with brown hair and green eyes, and incredibly he was smiling at her. "Miss Delaney, my name is Mike Nolan. I'm Nicholas Charron's chief of security. Mr. Charron would like to see you."

Confused, she glanced around, searching for the other two men, but they had vanished. "Look, Mr. Nolan, what's all this about? If it's the calculator, I'm sorry. I won't use it again."

Mike Nolan's smile remained the same, charming and easygoing, but Sydney suddenly realized that he was even more dangerous than the other men.

"I'm sure Mr. Charron will be glad to hear that. Now, if you'll allow me"—he took her arm and began guiding her through the crowd—"I'll take you to him."

Allowing didn't enter into it, and she knew it, Sydney reflected, not so much alarmed now as she was annoyed. She couldn't afford any delays in accomplishing her goal, and if she was about to be asked to leave the island, that would certainly throw a spanner into the works. There had to be some way out of the misunderstanding.

"Where exactly is it that you're taking me?" she asked as Mike Nolan halted before a set of black stainless steel doors and inserted a key.

"To Mr. Charron's suite."

The doors swished open, and they stepped into a lift. The doors closed, sealing her and the strange man by her side off from the comfort and familiarity of the crowd in the casino.

A trickle of alarm reentered her system. Along with curiosity. What kind of man would he be, she wondered, this man who had the power and wealth other men could only dream about? On his island he had fashioned a world to suit him, and within his world his power was absolute. For better or for worse, she was about to come face-to-face with Nicholas Charron, and much to her irritation, her heart was pounding at the prospect.

Three floors above ground level, the lift glided to a stop, the doors opened, and Sydney was facing the silent sanctuary of the owner of the Isle of Charron. A gentle push at the small of her back propelled her forward into the flowing expanse of the room. When she heard the doors close behind her, she wheeled, but the tall brown-haired man was no longer there. Amazing, she thought, how these men kept appearing and disappearing. Slowly she turned back to the room and began to walk forward.

She was truly lovely, Nicholas thought, watching her. Exquisite. Instinct had told him that she wasn't like the women he usually summoned to him, and he had been proved right. When she had first looked up and seen his men on either side of her, his theory had been confirmed. Her expression had changed from composure to fear. For an instant she had looked so defenseless that something like pain had twisted inside of him. To his mind, it hadn't seemed right that the first strong emotion he saw on her face should be fear. So he had called Mike.

The room, shadowed in dark drama and built on several levels, registered in Sydney's mind as a complete picture. Subdued indirect lighting was enhanced by gleaming surfaces and two mirrored walls. The other two walls were windows that seemed to carve a great space out of the midnight sky beyond and bring the night and the stars inside. Set about the room, tall white candles burned, their pale golden flames reflecting out from the dark windows and smoky mirrors, so that the flames appeared suspended, floating in the night. The sofas and chairs were rounded, their sensuous lines and curves covered with a pearlescent suede in a color that was somewhere between gray and black. On a beautifully carved table a crystal swan on a mirror lake.

The room was breathtaking, Sydney thought, but she couldn't shake the strange sensation that she was making her way through a rain forest, being stalked by a predatory animal.

She shrugged away the thought. Imagination could be a powerful thing. Too powerful. Judging that she must be in the center of the room, she came to a stop.

"Good evening."

She started at the deep voice. She hadn't even seen him, yet there he was! He was standing on a level above her, in front of a window, and for a moment she couldn't separate him from the night. They seemed as one.

As she had trained herself to do, she waited a beat before answering him. "Good evening."

Three long strides brought him down to her. "Thank you for coming."

"Did I have any choice?"

His mouth curved with humor. "Not really, but I won't apologize. I never apologize. Can I offer you something to drink?"

"No . . . thank you."

Like everything that surrounded him, his hair was dark, but candlelight picked up glints of silver that threaded through the black hair like streaks of moonlight. Sydney mentally shook herself. He was a man like any other. She had to stop equating him with the night. And she simply had to move away from him.

But his eyes were hypnotizing her. Dark brown, they appeared to have caught the flame of the candle as he looked at her. He was tall, lean, overpowering, and the formality of the tuxedo he wore emphasized his exotic appearance. But most disturbing of all, his masculinity seemed to generate an energy that she felt surrounding her. She had to remind herself that that couldn't be.

"Please, let me get you some refreshment. I have an excellent white wine I think you would like. It comes from my vineyards in the Barossa Valley near Adelaide."

Please, he had said. Like his men, he was extremely polite, but if she had thought they were dangerous, it was because she hadn't met their employer yet. He redefined the word.

She almost stuttered, but caught herself in time. "No. Thank you, anyway." If she kept her answers short, she would be okay.

"Then would you care to sit down?"

She chose the sofa because it was closest, and, as she did, noticed that the table in front of her was made of pale gray granite, probably from the Black Mountains near Cooktown.

The colors and textures of the room were a manifestation of the man—dark, hard, cool. Sydney was sure he hadn't needed a decorator. She imagined that he had just walked into the room, and it had taken shape around him.

As a result of her fantasizing, when he brought his long length down beside her, she was unprepared. His nearness enveloped her, and she could do nothing but wait for him to tell her why he had summoned her to his aerie.

She moved her head, and as the candlelight caught in her hair, suddenly the depth of tone Nicholas had seen on the monitor was explained. At first glance it appeared brown, but when the light touched it, her hair reflected the rich plum tones of a fine wine. "Are you enjoying your stay?"

The small talk was beginning to get on her nerves. "Very much. You have a beautiful island, Mr. Charron."

"Please, call me Nicholas . . . and I'll call you Sydney." When she made no comment, he continued. "Yes, the island is beautiful. I hope you'll be able to take full advantage of all our facilities while you're here."

She would have liked to have probed to discover why there was such a sardonic tone to his voice, but at the moment there were more important things to find out. "Mr. Charron, why have you had me brought up here?"

He bent his head to light a long brown cigarette, but he kept his eyes on her. "I wanted to meet you."

"You wanted to—then this isn't about the calculator?"

His mouth moved into what could have been a smile, but she wasn't sure. "You should have known better than to take out a calculator in full view of everyone, including my security men."

"I didn't know."

"What didn't you know?"

She could tell from his tone that he was amused. She had a deep-seated dislike—born out of a sensitive child's stutter—of being the source of anyone's amusement, but she forced herself to remain calm. "I didn't know that using a calculator was forbidden in a casino."

He took a draw on his cigarette, then exhaled a long stream of smoke, all the while observing her closely. "We have to take precautions against persons using a system."

"I wasn't using a system. As a matter of fact, I have yet to place a bet."

"I know."

"How do you know?"

"I've watched you." He smiled, because from the expression that passed briefly across her face, he could tell she hadn't thought he would admit it. And he smiled as he imagined his fingers weaving through the cascading waves of her luxuriant and soft hair. "You obviously aren't a professional gambler, Sydney. Do you know anything at all about gambling?"

"I'm learning."

Now that she was beside him, Nicholas could examine her skin closely. It was as if velvet had been put into a blender, whipped into a creamy froth, then poured over her, like icing. He wondered what creamed velvet would taste like.

His scrutiny had her clasping her hands tightly to still her nerves. "I didn't need to use the calculator anyway. It was just a crutch."

"Really? You didn't need to use the calculator? Tell me, then, what's the integral of X to the K power DX?"

"X to the K plus one power divided by K plus one, of course."

"Of course."

"Except when K equals minus one."

With her next heartbeat she realized she shouldn't have answered him. He obviously knew as much, if not more, mathematics as she, or he wouldn't have asked the question.

"What are you, Sydney Delaney?" he asked very softly. "Who are you?"

"I'm a guest at your resort, Mr. Charron, who's going to win a great deal of money from you."

He ground his cigarette into a crystal ashtray. "Really? How much?"

"Five hundred thousand dollars."

He didn't even blink. "Are you now?" Delicately, as a man might touch a shimmer of light from a moonbeam lest it dissolve beneath his hands, he stroked his fingers down the side of her throat. "I must be very careful not to bruise you."

Beneath his touch, heat surged within her. In her throat, words died.

His fingers moved to her lips and began outlining their soft shape . . . over . . . and over . . . and over. "Why do you want to win so much money, Sydney?"

She had declined his offer of wine, she thought hazily, but he was intoxicating her with his resonant voice, speaking caressing words that vibrated like a violin string within her. She knew if she spoke she would stutter and thus reveal the need welling inside her, so she remained silent.

"Do you gamble for the thrill of it?" His finger lingered in one soft corner of her mouth. "Or do you have a habit you're supporting—a man, a drug, a lifestyle?"

Feathering across the fullness of her bottom lip, his fingers seared her skin. Involuntarily her mouth opened. "Of the three, I hope it's a lifestyle" —his head began to lower toward her mouth— "because I couldn't allow you to be that involved with another man."

She couldn't breathe; she couldn't move. With smoke-textured words and a touch like fire, he was capably drawing her into a supersensory, black-velvet-lined realm where she could see only him, feel only him.

"And as for drugs," he murmured, "if you're going to be addicted to anything, it should be to me."

His words came to her with the heat and passion of a midnight wind, and his mouth closed on hers with such gentleness, she was disarmed, with such power, her usual command of her emotions was undermined.

She was being pulled into a morass of sensuality, and she was having trouble fighting against it. His tongue skimmed hers, then came back again to savor and to taste. Her blood heated, desire raced.

No matter what, she told herself, no matter how, she mustn't yield. Yet the pressure of his lips was increasing, setting off tiny bursts of fire all through her body. And his hands were on her back, sliding over her bare skin caressingly. Don't give in, she ordered herself. Don't give in!

Nicholas felt her resistance and ended the kiss. Pulling away, he regarded her with curiosity. The kiss had moved her every bit as much as it had moved him, he knew. Yet she hadn't surrendered completely. She had withheld her deepest response. Why?

Even now her eyes shimmered as if she were recalling their brief moments of shared passion. He, too, remembered, but he wanted more than moments. Much more. "Sydney Delaney," he murmured, "I don't know what's going on inside of you, but soon enough I will. Bet on it and you'll win."

"I—I—I must go," she said, coming to her feet, hoping he hadn't caught the stutter.

He stood also. "Have dinner with me tomorrow night."

She shook her head. "I—" She drew in a deep, relaxing breath. "I'll be busy."

"Doing what?"

"Nicholas, there's something you should understand. I didn't come here to enjoy myself. I came here to win a great deal of money, and that's going to take all my time and concentration."

He watched as she turned and walked to the lift. He waited until she pressed the button. Then he softly called, "Sydney?"

The doors opened before her, but at the sound of her name she looked over her shoulder.

He smiled. "You obviously think that I could cut into both your time and concentration. Thank you."

For a moment he thought she would say something, but she didn't. She entered the lift, and as she waited for the doors to close, she stood erect, her slim, gently curved body perfectly poised. Then the doors whooshed closed, and Nicholas was alone.

But in his mind the image of Sydney Delaney burned. And on his lips the taste of her lingered. And deep inside him his desire for her knotted.

Two

All her life Sydney had awakened early, first on Killaroo Station, and then when she had moved to Brisbane and taken the position with the bank. But last night she hadn't gotten back to her room until three, and she hadn't fallen asleep until five. Consequently, for the first time that she could remember, she had slept until noon.

It was now one o'clock, and although she had already dressed, she wasn't quite ready to venture out of her room. A few minutes before, room service, a rare luxury for her, had delivered coffee and a croissant, and now she lounged on the bed with her hands wrapped around a warm coffee cup. She had planned everything so carefully, but she hadn't factored Nicholas Charron into the equation. After her meeting with him, she felt the decided need to regroup her thoughts.

Thanks to her father, she had a great deal of confidence in herself, and that confidence extended into the area of men. She knew that men found her attractive, and she enjoyed their company in return. But although she dated frequently, no man had ever been able to break through the firm command she held over her emotions, and that was the way it would continue. Although last night in Nicholas's arms she had actually felt an urge to relinquish that command, she knew that she could not afford to allow the urge to resurface.

She didn't believe in living on the edge. There was no control on the edge. Nicholas Charron was the edge.

Taking a sip of coffee, she realized the solution to her problems was simple. She would avoid him. Fortunately it wouldn't be too difficult, considering he had a reputation as a recluse.

That decided, Sydney switched her thoughts to the reason she was on the Isle of Charron in the first place.

Because of her Irish Delaney blood, she believed in luck, but she also believed in skill and intelligence, and she had left no stone unturned in her preparation for her trip here. She had spent the previous month studying the subject of gambling.

As a junior officer of a respected bank, she had been able to save a nice nest egg, with the idea of one day being able to help her father. The time to help him had come sooner than she had expected, and although her savings weren't even close to the amount needed, it had been enough to finance her trip to the island and her betting over the next few weeks.

She had allotted a minimal amount of the money for travel, hotel, and meals, but the lion's share, approximately ten thousand dollars, had been set aside for gambling. She planned to risk only a certain amount each night, and if she lost it, she would stop and wait until the next evening. She believed in winning and losing streaks, and she had decided that on a night when she was losing, she wouldn't compound her bad luck by trying to recoup her losses. She would simply wait until the next night and try again.

Appropriate clothing hadn't proved to be a problem, since she had been working for six years and had accumulated a nice wardrobe. It was true that she didn't have a lot of resort wear, but because she had an active social life, she already had a few nice dresses suitable for evening, and it had been just a matter of prudently supplementing her wardrobe.

As for the actual process of gambling, she had spent the first few nights at the casino observing, weighing the pros and cons of each game. She had been blessed with the gift of photographic memory, and because of this gift, she had come to the conclusion that blackjack would be the game where she would have the greatest chance of achieving her goal. And she fully intended to achieve her goal. Tonight she would begin to put her knowledge to practical use.

She finished off the croissant and sat back, glancing around the room. A sea green satin coverlet lay at her feet on the bed, and on a table a large crystal bowl held an assortment of seashells and corals. It was the smallest, cheapest room the resort offered, yet it was still many times more luxurious than the average hotel room, and spotlessly clean.

But she hated walls, and suddenly these seemed closer than most; besides, inactivity bothered her. It was time to face the world, or at least, she amended with dry humor, the part that belonged to Nicholas Charron.

She grabbed her purse, let herself out of the room, and ran right into the Oriental man who had tried to take her to the security office the night before.

"Oh, I beg your pardon!" she exclaimed. "I didn't see you." Although he was slim and about an inch short of her own five-foot-six-inch height, she had felt his strength. Nevertheless, she couldn't help but worry. "Are you all right?"

On anyone less menacing, the expression that flitted briefly across his face might have been termed amusement. But without a word he bowed from the waist and moved on silently. Sydney's gaze followed him until he disappeared around a corner. What a strange little man, she thought, and one she certainly wouldn't want to meet in a dark alley at night.

As she made her way through the two-storied lobby, she saw very few people. It wasn't unusual, though, since she had found there wasn't much activity until four in the afternoon.

Walking toward the wide doorway, she admired the way the beauty of the island had been absorbed into the design of the lobby. Identical beds of bright red and blue flowers met at the glass walls and skimmed along both sides. And large rocks had been divided, half placed outside, half placed inside, so that a person couldn't be sure where the interior of the hotel stopped and the outdoors of the island began.

The front of the hotel faced the lee side of the island. Sydney headed down one of the crushed-coral paths, rimmed by exotic tropical flowers in colors so rich and vibrant they had to be one of life's miracles. To her left was a beautiful free-form swimming pool. Quite a few guests were lazing indolently beside it, though none seemed to have the energy to actually swim. Beyond the pool, tennis courts waited, empty of any players. Remembering Nicholas's sardonic tone of the night before when he had said that he hoped she would be able to take full advantage of their facilities, Sydney shook her head. He had provided every possible diversion for his guests, but few seemed inclined to take advantage of them.

She stopped and looked back at the hotel and casino complex—Charron's Glass Palace. The central portion rose three stories. Two-story wings on either side curved away from the main building, following the natural line of the island. She tilted her head, studying the glass structure that had been cleverly reinforced to withstand the tropical storms that each year slammed into the island. Reflected in the glass, the brilliant colors of the island seemed to melt together like an Impressionist painting. Nice trick, Mr. Charron, she saluted him silently.

A path cut off toward the right to trail through lush green vegetation overseen by tall pandanus. Sydney took the path, continuing until she came to the beach. Raising her hands, she shielded her eyes against the glare. In the distance the indigo-blue sea shimmered like windblown silk. Closer, as the waves broke over the reef that fringed this side of the island, the water turned calm and turquoise.

The beauty of it all was almost impossible to absorb in the short amount of time she had, and for a moment she wished she were here for a long vacation. But then she sighed, suddenly realizing that even the longest of holidays probably wouldn't give her enough time to appreciate this wondrous place.

She turned back and cut diagonally through the forest, making her way around to the side of the hotel. As she did, she thought she caught a brief glimpse of the second of the two men who had closed in on her so suddenly last night and frightened her, that big man whose face she had likened to Ayers Rock. An errant thought skittered through her mind, then was gone.

Her mind was too full of what she was about to see to be distracted for long. She had come this way each day since she had been here, and she had learned the path well. She didn't stop walking until she broke through the trees to the clearing and the lagoon.

There her footsteps ceased. Before her, black swans glided serenely on a turquoise lagoon. As a child she had pored over books that contained pictures of black swans, but until she had come to the Isle of Charron, she had never actually seen any.

The birds had always seemed magical to her—so beautiful and wild. So free. And now they didn't disappoint her. They were the most enchanting creatures she had ever seen. They enthralled her as they swam silently, regally, among the reeds.

She chose a spot, crossed her legs, and sank to the ground.

Although it was true that the Isle of Charron was the closest legalized casino to her home in Brisbane, she supposed she could have managed to go to the one in Alice Springs. Or there was the one in Darwin, although it was probably the farthest, and then there were the two in Tasmania. But the reputation of big money being won and lost at Charron's Glass Palace had been only a small part of the lure to the island.

She hadn't been able to resist the black swans of Charron. They were the real reason she had chosen to come here. They were a part of her childhood dreams.

She remembered that at first she had been unsure of her chances of being able to stay at the resort. An obstacle had been its exclusivity. It had been only by the greatest stroke of good luck that a reservation for a single room had opened up. She had taken it on the spot.

From her position she could hear the murmur of the sea and the waters of the lagoon lapping at her feet. Somewhere overhead a silver gull called out. Nearby a big blue butterfly floated above a scarlet canna flower. Sounds and sights of nature, infinitely peaceful, boundlessly soothing.

A twig snapping behind her represented an intrusion into that peace. Twisting around, she caught sight of the Ayers Rock man, lurking in the brush. Sydney jumped to her feet, equal portions of fear and anger lodging in her throat. "W-w-why are you following me?"

At first she thought he would disappear back into the forest, but he lumbered out.

"Answer me!"

"Orders, Miss Delaney."

"Whose?" she asked, although she didn't need to.

He hesitated, gazing away as if he were embarrassed to look her in the face. "I really can't say."

"Then take me to someone who can."

Obediently he turned onto the coral path and she followed. Her only surprise was that the office the big man led her into was Mike Nolan's, not Nicholas Charron's.

When she entered the office, the chief of security's head was bent over a stack of paperwork, but as soon as he saw her, he stood up, smiling that charming, easygoing smile of his. "Miss Delaney, how nice to see you. You've rescued me." He waved his hand over the pile of work on his desk. "This is the part of the job I hate the most."

"Mr. Nolan, why am I being followed?"

"Ah." He nodded his head knowingly. "You discovered Julian. That explains the look of outrage on your face. Julian is losing his touch. He's never been detected before."

"Julian?" she repeated, absorbing the name with some disbelief.

"The big man who brought you here. I think he's developed a crush on you. He was telling me just this morning how beautiful he thinks you are."

She didn't believe him for a moment. People who looked like Ayers Rock didn't say things like that. Sydney stared at him stonily. "I repeat, Mr. Nolan, why am I being followed?"

He walked around his desk until he was in front of it, then leaned back against the walnut surface. "I'm extremely thankful to be able to tell you that the sole responsibility is Nicholas's."

She had known that already, and she refused to be swayed by Mike's twinkling green eyes. "I asked you *why*. What could I possibly have done to lead anyone to believe that I'm dangerous?"

His smile widened. "Good question."

Her brows drew together in temper. "What exactly were your orders?"

"That you were not to be allowed to leave the island."

Her hands balled into fists. She lived her life within boundaries of control, but they were her *own* boundaries, no one else's. Did Nicholas possibly think that their meeting last night had so unnerved her that she would run?

The ice in her voice would have shaken a less assured man. "Tell Mr. Charron that it would take more than one encounter with him to make me leave before I'm ready."

He eyed her with interest. "Why don't you tell him yourself?"

It took a minute before she could control the jump of her nerves. It hadn't been that long ago that she had told herself she was going to avoid Nicholas Charron. "Fine. Where is he?"

"Sleeping. He sleeps until about sundown. But

you can tell him tonight over dinner. He's usually here by nine."

"Here? You mean he sleeps somewhere else?"

"Most nights he goes to his place over on the other side of the island, the wilder side. It suits Nick, and it's inaccessible to his guests."

"I see." During the day Nicholas slept on the wild side of the island. And at night he roamed his glass palace like a panther in a rain forest. "Well, Mr. Nolan—"

"Mike, please."

Why not? she thought with resignation. It looked as if she were fated to get to know Nicholas Charron's security men well. "Mike, call off the watchdogs, including the little one."

"Little one? Oh, you mean Sai."

"Sai," she repeated with a roll of her eyes. "You have my word that when I leave the island, I won't sneak away. That's just not my way, and if Mr. Charron knew me better, he'd realize it."

"I think getting to know you better is what he has in mind, Sydney, and I'm going to hold you to your word. The value of my life would go down a great deal if I let you slip away."

"How amazing," she said faintly.

He shrugged. "Nick is an amazing man."

He was there again, up in the control room, watching her. Sydney's nerves had told her the exact time he had arrived. Surreptitiously she glanced at her watch. Eight-thirty. Earlier tonight she had pulled her hair back and up into a shining knot on top of her head. Now she raised her hand to the back of her neck, where it felt as if the tiny hairs were raised.

She had been gambling for several hours, engrossed in the play at the blackjack table, when suddenly she had sensed his eyes on her. This time she did question how she had known he was there. How could that be? An uncanny awareness seemed to link them, a thread of sensuality that stretched between them with the inevitability and power of the tides.

Sydney attempted to bring her attention back to the action at the table. She had been winning and losing about equally, but she wasn't overly worried. She wasn't playing the big stakes yet. She considered this the learning period.

There were three other players beside herself, and the dealer had just shuffled two hands ago, using four decks. The dealer's upcard was an ace. She looked down at her hand. She had an eight and a nine. Without thinking about it, she indicated to the dealer that she wanted a hit. The dealer dealt her a four. Twenty-one.

The groan from the man beside her barely registered, because she was too busy berating herself. She should never have called for that hit. The dealer folded. It didn't matter. Winning had been pure luck, because Nicholas had broken her concentration. She collected her chips and pushed back from the blackjack table, deciding to give herself a break.

But first . . . With deliberate defiance she raised her eyes to the mirrored wall where she knew he stood, intent on showing him that his presence meant nothing to her. But her defiant gesture boomeranged, for she could feel his gaze on her as if it were his very touch searing her. And she had the sure feeling that if she raised her hand to the shimmering air between them, her hand would come away scorched by the heat.

Shaken, she turned and walked quickly out of the casino.

Her destination was the main lift. She intended to slip up to her room for a few minutes, but at the lift doors she found Mike lazily leaning against the wall, his long, lean body blocking the button.

She eyed him suspiciously and earned one of his easygoing smiles. In her peripheral vision she caught a blonde watching him. Mike Nolan was indeed a devastating man.

"Nicholas wants to see you."

Her temper began to rise. "And he sent you to ask me?"

"That's right."

"Mike, I happen to know that he has two perfectly good legs, and last night he seemed to have no trouble talking. Why doesn't he ask me himself?"

"He prefers to do it this way."

"Tell me, Mike, don't you find it a trifle kinky to procure women for your boss?"

She had meant to be deliberately inciteful, but he took it good-naturedly. "Not really. Most of the time, getting women for Nick is so cut and dried, it's rather boring. He just tells me who he wants, I relay the message, and the woman in question agrees."

She couldn't believe what she was hearing. "Cut and dried?"

"Sydney," he said gently, "the women he invites up to his suite get exactly what they want—a chance to sleep with the notorious Nicholas Charron."

"Why did you tell me that?"

A puzzled look crossed his handsome face, and all at once he laughed. "I'm not sure."

Learning to like Mike was draining a portion of her anger away, but not all. "In case there's the slightest doubt in your mind, I'm not one of the women who wants to sleep with him."

"Oh, I know that, but I don't think what you want will matter all that much ultimately."

Suddenly, Sydney felt stifled, and she experienced the desperate urge to be alone for a while. "Mike, did you happen to see the pretty redhead who's playing at the roulette table tonight?"

His green eyes danced. "Of course."

"Tell Mr. Charron to try his luck with her. I'm willing to bet she'll run, not walk, to him." With that biting statement she reached behind him and forcibly punched the lift button.

Moments later she was putting her key into the lock and letting herself into her room. She extended her hand to the lamp on the dresser and clicked it on.

Light blazed in a small and bright halo, brilliant at the center, but diffusing as it reached to the edges of the room and touched the single chair and the man who sat in it—Nicholas Charron.

She almost stammered. She almost asked, How

did you get in here? but she caught herself in time and did neither. She tossed her bag onto the dresser. "I'm aware that you own this hotel, Nicholas, but surely it's unethical to let yourself into a room one of your guests is occupying."

"Ethics have never bothered me overly much." He came up out of the chair to cross the room and stand before her. "And I like the way you say *Nicholas.*" He touched her cheek softly. "You're angry with me."

His touch sent warmth rushing through her. She ignored it. "How do you know that? You couldn't possibly have had time to talk to Mike. I just left him."

"I saw the look you gave me from the casino floor. You have spirit, Sydney Delaney."

"And you have no manners, Nicholas Charron. Where do you get off sending for a woman as if she were some item on the room service menu?"

"In the past, that's all it has meant to me."

His stark honesty took her breath away.

"In the past," he repeated softly. "With you, there's a brand-new slate just begging to be written on, and I can't wait to begin."

An emotion she couldn't label clogged her throat to the point that she had to clear it before she spoke. "Why?"

"When I find out, I'll let you know."

"I won't be sent for, Nicholas, and I won't be continuously watched."

"Solve the problem, Sydney. *Stay with me.*"

She had never known such a frustrating man, or such an exciting man. She had to fight against her stutter. "Do you always do exactly as you please?"

"Always." While she pondered his answer he pushed his hands into his pockets and threw an idle glance around the room. "This is one of our smallest rooms. I don't think I ever realized how small until I sat here, waiting for you."

"It's fine for my purposes."

"Purposes? I suppose you're talking about winning the five hundred thousand dollars."

She nodded, trying to calculate if she could make it around him to the other side of the room without brushing against him. She decided she couldn't, so she stayed where she was, willing her composure back into place.

"I'll make you a deal. Tell me why you want five hundred thousand dollars, and I'll never again send for you."

Unexpectedly she smiled, a smile as lovely and as secretive as Mona Lisa's, a smile that told him nothing but tempted him to move mountains to find out the secrets held within that smile. Her smile stunned him almost as much as what she said next.

"I'll tell you this much, the money is for a man."

He moved away.

Relief that he was no longer so close to her quickly faded as he reached his long arm across the bed and picked up the nightgown she had laid out earlier. Pale gold in color, it slid across his hands with sensuous ease.

The color would make her skin lustrous, Nicholas thought. And if a man ran his hands across her skin to the silk gown, he would hardly know where material began and skin stopped.

"Tell me, Sydney, why five hundred thousand dollars? Why not six or four?"

The pale gold of her gown against the burnished copper skin-tone of his hands had her swallowing hard. The sight of such a hard, masculine man holding such a feminine garment—hers—set her nerves quivering with an excitement that she had trouble banking down.

"I've told you all I intend to on that subject. It's a private matter."

He held up the gown, put his face into it, and inhaled. When he raised his head, his eyes were almost black. "You smell like flowers at dawn that are just beginning to open their petals to the sensual warmth of the day."

Heat in her lower limbs made her legs go weak. She told herself that she had to do something to regain control of the situation. "How would you know what flowers smell like at dawn? I understand you never see the sun. You come out only at night, like some . . . some sort of vampire."

He laughed warmly, fully. Then he crossed to her and wrapped the nightgown around her neck so that she could feel its silken smoothness on the exposed nape. "The truth is, I like the night. Everything is gentler, more muted at night. Scars are less easily seen at night."

Using the nightgown, he slowly pulled her body forward until her breasts were pressed against his chest and her stomach was experiencing the pressure of the hard muscles of his lower abdomen. "But there's also something else you need to consider, Sydney, because maybe there could be another truth at work here. Maybe I *am* a vampire. Maybe I need to drink from your innocence and your passion to live." His next words were murmured barely above a whisper. "If you find that *is* the truth, what will you do? Will you run?"

Silk . . . silk around her neck . . . words spoken with the sensuality of silk . . . his breath as soft as silk on her mouth. It was too much for her. "N-n-no. O-o-of course not."

A strange light came and went in his eyes, but Sydney didn't see it. Her eyes were on his lips, and when they touched hers, she began to ache deeply, exquisitely.

Nicholas's head swam with her closeness. His body told him to take quickly. But his mind remembered her stutter, and a tenderness he had never before used with a woman took over. The nightgown slipped from his hands as he tempered his passion; he withheld his strength, and instead, with his lips, with his tongue, let the desire flow slowly and softly. He didn't attempt to swamp her with his finesse. And a floodtide of sweetness came rushing back at him.

Sweet passion. It was something he had never before experienced. It was a sweetness that he would enjoy savoring . . . for a week . . . for a month . . . maybe even longer.

"N-N-Nicholas."

He lifted his head and looked down at her. With the effects of his kiss still on her lips, she appeared even more beautiful. But her eyes held a wounded look and he understood. He understood so much now.

She walked as far away from him as the size of the room would allow. "You shouldn't have done that." There was a slight quiver in her voice, but if he heard it, he gave no indication.

Instinctively he knew that if he gave ground now, he would never get it back. "You mean kiss you?" He reached into his pocket and pulled out a cigarette. Taking his time, he lit it. "Why not? It was very nice. I enjoyed it. You enjoyed it."

"I—"

"You what, Sydney? You didn't enjoy it? There's simply no way you'll make me believe that. So tell me something else."

With shaking fingers she attempted to smooth her hair back into place, pushing at it in annoyance until she finally gave up.

"Th-th-that's just it, Nicholas! Words don't seem to mean anything to you. Or maybe I should change that to *I* don't say the words that make you listen."

Regarding her steadily, he took a final drag on the cigarette and crushed it out. Then he came to her and with a practiced motion swept all the pins from her hair until the glossy, plum-colored mass came tumbling down around her shoulders. "What is it, Sydney, that you think I want to hear?"

"You want to hear *yes*."

"Oh, you'll say yes to me, Sydney. There's not a doubt in my mind. You'll cry yes. You'll shout yes. And it will be soon."

"H-h-hasn't any woman ever said no to you, Nicholas?"

He smiled. "Before you there have been no other women."

"Now it's my turn to tell you that I don't believe you. It's well known that—"

"Everything you've ever heard about me is probably true, Sydney. I want you to know that now."

She shook her head. "Y-y-you say the most extraordinary things. I don't know what to believe."

He took her face between his hands and looked deep into her golden eyes. "Believe this. I will kiss you again . . . and again . . . and again. And then you will ask me for more."

Three

Three nights had passed since Sydney had found Nicholas waiting in her room. At times she knew he was above her in his control room, watching her, but she was learning to handle his surveillance without letting it bother her too much. In some ways his unseen presence helped her, perhaps because she felt she had something to prove to him—that he didn't affect her concentration and that she was indeed going to win five hundred thousand dollars from his casino.

But whatever the reason, she could actually concentrate on her gambling now, and the best part was that she was winning larger and larger amounts. She was pleased. Her plan was going well.

Only a very small part of her wondered why Nicholas had decided to leave her alone. And she tried to convince herself it was merely mild curiosity that made her want to know.

• • •

Mike entered the control room and shut the door behind him. His eyes searched out and found the dark man who had been his friend for most of his adult life standing by the monitors. He crossed to stand beside him.

Mike didn't need to check the screen to know whom Nicholas was watching. "How's the beautiful Sydney this evening?"

Nicholas took a moment to light a cigarette. "Beautiful."

"That she is. Men are standing in line to gamble at whichever table she chooses. I'm afraid one of these nights I'm going to have a fight on my hands."

Nicholas's lips barely curved into a smile. With the hand that held his cigarette he gestured toward her. "She's winning."

"She told you she would."

"Sydney's good. She's very good and getting better every night. I just wish . . ."

"You just wish what? That she were like so many other women who have fallen into your arms for a night, then left the next morning with barely a protest? No, you don't."

Nicholas shot Mike a narrow look, then grinned reluctantly. Taking advantage of Nicholas's momentary attention, Mike said, "Mandarin's out."

The grin left his face with a suddenness that would have shocked anyone else but Mike. "Where is she?"

"Hong Kong."

Nicholas's gaze returned to the monitor that showed a full view of the table where Sydney sat. "Is Mandarin all right?"

"She's fighting an infection she picked up in that hellhole of a prison. But word is that soon she'll be coming for you."

Nicholas smiled, this time without humor. "I didn't expect anything less of her. Does she know yet that Josh is dead?"

"I don't know, but I want you to listen to me. I've beefed up security, and I expect you to cooperate. As long as you stay on the island, I can protect you."

"Why bother trying? Mandarin's had ten years to plan her revenge. She'll succeed."

A young man appeared at Mike's side. Mike took a clipboard from him and scrawled his name across the bottom of the paper that was attached to it. Handing it back with a dismissive nod, he waited until the young man was out of earshot. "You lived in the East too long, Nick. There's a streak of fatalism in you."

"I am a part of all I have seen."

"I was there with you, remember?"

This time the humor came up behind Nicholas's smile. "Thank God you were. We had some exciting times."

"Yeah. I have to admit that I miss it sometimes. This is all rather tame compared. Although"—his eyes lit up at the sight of a petite blonde just walking into the casino—"it does have its benefits."

Nicholas chuckled and moved to the wide sheet of one-way mirror. "I just know you're speaking of the Great Barrier Reef."

"Of course I am." His eyes stayed on the blonde as she threaded her way through the crowd, finally stopping at the bar that was separated from the area where the actual gambling took place. When Mike at last looked away from the monitor and spoke, his tone was thoughtful. "But how about you, old friend? You have the power and the money to live exactly as you want, but don't you ever miss it all? The adventure? The danger?"

Nicholas's gaze rested briefly on Mike before returning to the casino floor below and to Sydney Delaney. "Not really. I put my time in with the human race. And for now at least, I choose to bring only select parts of the world to me. Until lately . . ."

Mike followed Nicholas's gaze. "Until lately, what?"

With a quickness of movement that Mike had never gotten used to, Nicholas wheeled from the window and headed for the door. "Nick, where are you going?" Mike called. "*Nicholas!* Where are you going?"

"Sydney hates to be sent for, so I'm going to her."

Mike gazed after Nicholas, utter astonishment written on his face. "He's going to her? Well, I'll be damned!"

The impact of Nicholas's presence rushed through the casino like a tidal wave, growing stronger and picking up speed as person after person turned to stare at his progress across the room.

Sydney became aware that something unusual was happening when the competent, deft hands of her dealer faltered, then ceased their motion altogether. Glancing up in puzzlement, she found the young man's mouth had dropped open. Unable to resist, she twisted around to see if she could find out what had so stunned the usually unflappable dealer.

Her gaze collided with that of Nicholas's, and unable to control it, her heart leaped. Of course, she thought. She should have known. And she should have admitted to herself that she had been waiting for him. . . .

"Good evening, Sydney. Winning some more of my money, I see."

"I'm trying. What are you doing?"

"I'm about to ask you to have dinner with me." As if he had just become aware of the attention his appearance had caused, he lasered a glance around the room, sending his dealers back to their work.

Sydney couldn't help but smile at the reaction Nicholas commanded. The power of the man was evident, and in a room where there were a number of tuxedos, he wore his tuxedo with an ease and sophistication that made him stand out. "Isn't this a little out of your neighborhood, Nicholas?"

His dark brown eyes became fixed on her mouth. "You know, if Leonardo DaVinci were alive today, he would send Mona Lisa home and paint you instead."

"R-r-really?" Oh, hell! she thought. Why did he have to say such extraordinary things?

In response to a barely seen motion of Nicholas's hand, Sai materialized before them, seemingly from nowhere. "Cash Miss Delaney out and credit her account."

Sydney cast Nicholas a surprised look. "But I'm not ready to quit playing!"

He leaned toward her and said softly, "Come on, let me take you to dinner while I've still got some money."

She found the curve of his lips awfully attractive, and suddenly she was in an exceedingly good mood. After all, he had come to her instead of sending for her; and she had been winning a great deal of his money and planned to win more. Why not go to dinner? she asked herself, all the while knowing exactly why she shouldn't. The man represented a danger to her.

"Where?"

"That's up to you. We have three restaurants to choose from, or we could go upstairs to the suite."

Some choice, she thought, allowing humor to enter into the situation—a nervous stomach caused by eating alone with him, or a nervous stomach caused by curious people watching them eat. At least, though, he had given her a choice.

"I don't fancy being the brunt of people's stares. Let's eat in your suite."

Sydney wondered if Nicholas always had candles lit, and she wondered about the other women who had sat where she was sitting. She wondered how many there had been, and she wondered if he had made them feel as special as he was making her feel.

The dining area was three levels up from the main floor. The table at which they dined was next to the window and was inlaid with onyx and rimmed with malachite; the surface of the table was polished to such a high degree that everything reflected off it as if the table were a still pond.

She let her gaze drift around the rest of the room, and almost immediately her attention was caught by the crystal swan she had noticed the first time she had been in the room.

She nodded toward the piece. "You moved the swan. The other night it was on the table by the wall."

He paused in the act of pouring himself another glass of wine. "That's right. How did you remember that?"

She didn't want to admit to having a photographic memory, because she didn't want to get into the subject of how she was using it to help her win at blackjack. "It's unusual, and I have a good memory."

He regarded her steadily. "Do you?"

"It's truly beautiful, but I have to admit that I like your black swans more."

He set the wine bottle down. "Then you've been to see them?"

"Every afternoon. I've grown very attached to them. They're the first black swans I've ever seen other than in picture books. When I was a little girl, it was a fantasy of mine to actually see them fly." She smiled self-consciously. "I suppose it was because we didn't have any black swans where I grew up."

"And where was that?"

"On a sheep station called Killaroo."

"Really? Tell me, what's it like to grow up on a sheep station?"

She laughed. "It was wonderful. My two sisters and I considered Killaroo our own private wonderland. We were constantly finding new and exciting things to do. I have two truly extraordinary sisters. Manda can talk anybody into anything, and Addie doesn't even have to try. Her mere presence is enough to cause people to fall under her spell."

"It stands to reason that you'd have remarkable sisters, since you're so unique yourself."

"Me?"

"You don't see it, do you?" he murmured. "You have my men ready to kill for you. And since you've been at the casino, the house odds have increased dramatically. No man within ten feet of you can keep his mind on gambling. Your beauty stuns, Sydney, while your innocence draws."

His dark gaze rested on her with remarkable possession, and she reacted. "I'm not an innocent."

"Compared to me you are."

"Something tells me that compared to you the Marquis de Sade would be an innocent." The minute she said it, she knew it was a bad joke, and she wished with all her heart for the ability to take the words back.

With great gentleness he took her hand. "I've already told you that everything you've ever heard about me is true, Sydney, but try not to judge me too harshly."

Had there been a trace of pain in his voice, she wondered, or had it been her imagination working overtime again? "I'm not judging you at all, Nicholas. I apologize if you think I was. To be truthful, I haven't heard that much"—she shrugged—"rumors, that's all."

"Good. Good." Nicholas relaxed back into his chair. "So tell me about your exciting adventures on Killaroo."

Because of the pain she thought she had heard in his tone, she told him some things she had told very few people. "You know, it's funny, but when I remember my childhood, it's the little things that are the most vivid to me. For instance, I remember how the lanolin from the sheep's wool during shearing time would make my father's hands so wonderfully soft. And I remember sitting in a small room with my two sisters doing our lessons while we listened to *School of the Air* over the radio. I remember how my mother's laughter used to remind me of music." She laughed herself, making the dark man across from her tilt his head in order to catch the sound. "Oh, and yes! I remember my father teaching me to throw a boomerang."

Nicholas interrupted. "You can throw a boomerang?"

"I sure can, and quite well too."

"I'm impressed."

Her golden eyes sparkled with laughter. "Are you? I'm not sure I thought that was possible. I feel like I've accomplished something monumental."

Nicholas's lips curved appreciatively. He couldn't remember the last time he had enjoyed himself more. Sydney's enthusiasm for her family and her home was a tangible thing, and as she talked, she unknowingly was throwing out sparks of light and life, weaving a tapestry of warm emotions around him. To be caught up in someone else was unusual for him, and he found he didn't want her to stop. "Go on. What else do you remember?"

"Well, I do have one very special memory."

"Tell me."

She smiled, recalling, "One magical night, my sisters and I sneaked out of bed and out of the house to witness a corroboree the Aborigines who worked for us were putting on. We weren't supposed to be there, of course, but we had heard whispers of the celebration, and we decided we couldn't miss it." Sydney leaned forward with her forearms on the table. "The night was absolutely glorious, the moon was full, and the three of us had all the energy and enthusiasm of the very young. We hid in deep shadows by the base of a giant banyan tree. The night was full of primitive sounds, but it never occurred to us to be afraid. In the middle of a circle of fires, the Aborigines, their bodies painted with ochre, danced and chanted. Even as young as we were, it was a deeply stirring experience for the three of us to witness a ritual that was as old as time itself. We watched them for hours until we fell asleep."

"Under the banyan tree?"

"That's right. The next thing I remember, I opened my eyes and the night seemed to be moving around me. I felt strong arms holding me, and I knew I was being carried back to the house by my father. I fell back asleep before we got there, though, and the next morning my sisters and I woke in our own beds."

"Safe and sound."

She nodded. "But I still remember that night as if it were yesterday."

His voice was soft. "Sounds like you have a lot of good memories."

"Yes." She tilted her head to one side and regarded him. "Don't you?"

He stuck one of his long brown cigarettes between his teeth, flicked a slim gold lighter, and put the flame to the tip. "Not as many as you have probably. I grew up on the streets of Chicago, a pretty tough little kid. I had to be. My family was quite poor, and we had very little."

"But you must have one good memory," she said, prodding him. "Something?"

He took a moment to study her, and Sydney recognized the look on his face. She had seen it many times on the faces of men as they tried to calculate the odds of a game.

"Yes, I have one," he said slowly. "One bitterly cold day I was walking along the street, when something in a store window caught my attention. It was a figurine of a beautiful young girl. I can still remember how cold that glass pane felt as I pressed my face against it, trying to see better. I was awestruck. That young girl made of porcelain represented everything unattainable to me at that time in my life—beauty, gentleness, and a fragility that cried out to me. You remind me of that figurine."

Disconcerted, she tried to speak too quickly. "B-b-but why?"

"Because of the qualities I've already mentioned. And because she had a perfect grace of stillness, and so do you. And because she had a glass dome protecting her, and so do you."

"I—I—I . . ." She stopped, upset with herself that he could make her expose her stutter. She gave herself a moment, then spoke again. "I have no glass dome protecting me." As a matter of fact, she thought, around Nicholas, she found herself less and less protected.

"Actually, Sydney, there's a shimmering life beneath your stillness, along with a fire. And for a few minutes, while you were talking about your family and Killaroo, you came out from under your glass dome, and I was able to see what it might have been like if that porcelain doll had come alive all those years ago. Seeing you like that has made me determined. I intend to bring you out from under that glass dome, gradually at first, but then more and more, until you can do away with it completely."

"I—I—I don't know what you're talking about."

"It's that control of yours," he said with a softness meant to seduce. "And it's so unnecessary."

She fought against the seduction in his voice. She fought against the warmth in his dark brown eyes. But she had the feeling she was losing, until a discreet knock on the door interrupted the silence that had fallen between them.

Nicholas went to answer the door. It was Julian, and the big man wheeled in a cart with a coffee service and an assortment of desserts. Just inside the door he paused, fished in the pocket of his jacket, and pulled out a note. "Mike said you should have this right away. It just came."

As Nicholas read the note, Julian wheeled the

cart to the table. "Sorry to interrupt, Miss Delaney, but I told the waiter I'd bring the coffee in."

Sydney had grown used to Julian. And without making the mistake of discounting his menacing facade, she had come to see the shyness that lurked beneath. She smiled. "That's very nice of you, Julian."

Her smile appeared to startle him. With his attention still focused on her, he lifted a large hand for the coffeepot and tilted it until coffee began to pour from the spout. *Onto the tray.* "Oh, hell!" He slammed the silver pot down, and reached for a napkin. "Please excuse me, Miss Delaney. I'm sorry."

"Don't worry about it. Can I help?" She reached out her hand toward him, and it so alarmed him that his hand jerked and knocked both coffee cups to the floor, where the china shattered.

"Damn! Oh!" He was stricken. "Please excuse my language, Miss Delaney, it won't happen again." He dropped to the floor and began quickly picking up the pieces.

"Be careful, Julian! Oh, no!"

A bright spurt of blood appeared on his hand. "Here"—she grabbed a clean linen napkin and knelt beside him—"don't move, Julian. You're hurt."

"I'm fine, Miss Delaney." He cast a helpless glance over her shoulder at Nicholas. "I need to clean up the mess."

Wrapping the napkin around his hand, she said, "Don't be silly. You've got to be still, Julian, or you're going to make it worse." Her brow wrinkled with worry. "It's a deep cut. I think you're going to need stitches. Nicholas?"

"Yes, Sydney?"

"Does the Isle of Charron have a doctor?"

"Yes, as a matter of fact we do. He's extremely underworked, but nevertheless very good."

She smiled into Julian's face with encouragement. "There, you see. Now, I want you to go to the doctor right away and then give me a ring and let me know you're all right."

"Uh, Miss Delaney, I don't think . . ."

Nicholas reached down for Sydney's arm and pulled her to her feet. "I think arguing with Miss Delaney is useless, Julian. Why don't you just go on down and see the doctor?"

Julian raised his huge bulk off the floor, nodded to Sydney, and left.

As soon as the door shut, Nicholas broke into laughter.

Sydney turned to him bewildered. "What's wrong?"

"You just sent one of the toughest men I've ever known to the doctor for a minor cut."

"I-i-it wasn't minor! It was bleeding quite a lot."

"Sydney, that man once dug a bullet out of his own leg and didn't let anyone know until the next day." He chuckled. "Bemusement is an expression I don't think Julian's face has ever worn before."

"He was hurting!"

"And that's the key, isn't it, Sydney?"

"I—I—I don't know what you mean."

"You saw someone you thought was hurting and vulnerable and you rushed to help him without thought for yourself. Do you realize that you didn't stutter once the whole time you were talking to him? Nor did you guard against it."

"I d-d-don't want to talk about my s-s-stutter."

"Shhh." He pressed a finger to her lips. "Let's go sit on the couch. Would you like some coffee? I can ring for more cups."

Mutely she shook her head.

"Would you like anything?" When she didn't answer, he took the cushion beside her. "Don't be embarrassed, Sydney. I find your stutter endearing."

Her golden brown eyes flashed the anger she was feeling. "Y-y-you can't possibly understand! Wanting to speak so badly, *needing* to speak, but being afraid to open your mouth for fear of not being able to say what you want . . . for fear of making a f-f-fool of yourself."

Her anger didn't faze him, because he knew he wasn't going to let her out of his sight until it had dissolved. "I understand fear, Sydney. And more and more I understand you. When I first heard your stutter, it answered a lot of questions that I had had about you." With a finger he lifted her chin so that she would look at him. "You appeared so controlled. Even when I kissed you, you didn't respond completely. But I knew your emotions weren't frozen. Beneath your surface runs fire. And it's a fire I've just got to have."

Even though he hadn't moved toward her, he was about to kiss her. She knew it. She could feel it. "Leave me alone, Nicholas."

"I'll give you anything you want, Sydney, but not that."

She took a deep, steadying breath and moved on the offensive. "So okay, then, satisfy my curiosity. You talk about my control, and you've compared me to a figurine who lives under a glass dome. But what about you, Nicholas? You live a life that is every bit as controlled as mine, maybe even more so. You're a man who keeps himself apart from people, watching them from behind a glass wall. Why is that?"

"I haven't noticed that I've been keeping myself apart from you, Sydney."

"I-i-is that right? Well, I don't remember seeing you for the last few nights, do I?"

With a fingertip he feathered a tiny plum-colored curl. "It's a funny thing, Sydney. Life has taught me to be a man of great patience, but in your case, I find patience to be almost impossible. I had thought perhaps that a couple of nights away from you might lessen the urgency of my desire for you. I was wrong."

Oh, yes, Sydney thought. Her first instincts about him had been right. The man was danger personified. Allowing a bit of what she was feeling to show, she shook her head. "You totally overwhelm me, Nicholas."

"No, I don't. You have beauty and strength, Sydney, and you have passion. The problem is you've been chained to the ground by your stammer for far too long. You just have to free that passion in order to break those chains. Then together we'll be able to soar."

She couldn't ignore the sexual challenge he had thrown out, nor could she ignore the way the atmosphere had suddenly become charged. She felt as if she were being pulled toward him. Abruptly panic erupted inside her, because she knew that she wanted to go into his arms more than anything in the world.

It came to him so easily, she thought—controlling the atmosphere, controlling people, this attempt of his to control her mind and her body.

No!

She had to leave. Now.

Hurriedly she got up. "M-m-my stutter is something I've lived with my whole life, Nicholas, and despite it I've done very well. I need to get back down to the casino now."

He allowed her to reach the doors of the lift before he spoke. "Sydney?"

As always, his voice stopped her, and she turned.

"Have you ever been down to the lagoon at sunset? You really must go. It's a beautiful sight."

"Good night, Nicholas."

"Good night, Sydney."

Four

"Don't worry, Addie. I'll be there as soon as I can. 'Bye for now." Sydney hung up the phone and rolled out of bed, her mind working fast and furiously. Addie had said she needed her to come at once, and that meant she had a lot to do.

Sydney glanced at the clock. Eight A.M. If Addie had wondered why her sister was still in bed at such a late hour, she hadn't said a word, but then, that was just like Addie.

A short time later, Sydney was dressed and packed and facing the problem of how to get off the island. She had promised Mike that if she ever left the island, she wouldn't just sneak away, and she meant to keep the promise. But whom could she notify? she wondered. She was sure that Nicholas was sleeping at his retreat over on the other side of the island. That left Mike.

But once downstairs, she could find no sign of Mike. She inquired at the desk for him, but the young woman who was on duty wasn't able to help, though she did tell Sydney that the first launch leaving the island wasn't until one o'clock.

Sydney made her way out onto the terrace and found Sai sitting in a corner having a cup of coffee.

She rushed over to him. "Sai, you've got to help me! Where's Mike?"

Sai rose, his black eyes regarding her enigmatically.

"Please, Sai. I-i-it's very important. I must talk to Mike."

The small man seemed to hesitate, but then he bowed from the waist and began to lead the way toward one of the wings. Used to Sai's silent ways by now, Sydney followed him. When he stopped in front of a door, she cast him a quizzical glance. "Is this Mike's room?"

Sai bowed again, so Sydney raised her hand and knocked. There was no answer. She waited a minute and knocked again. When another minute had passed and no one came to the door, she looked at Sai. "Are you sure he's in there?"

Again Sai bowed. With a sigh, Sydney knocked one more time. "Sai, he's not answering. He must be asleep. I've got to get in there."

Without a word, Sai withdrew a ring of keys from his pocket and inserted one of the keys into the door. Then he opened it and stepped aside.

With a nod of gratitude to him, Sydney entered what appeared to be a living area. The curtains were still drawn, and what light there was in the room was dim. But she could see that the room was empty. Without debating the matter, she headed for the door that she assumed was the bedroom.

Knocking lightly on the door, she called, "Mike?" and listened carefully. Convinced that she heard something, she turned the knob and walked in. But the room was dark and all she could see was a mound of covers on the bed. Well, if she had to wake Mike up, Sydney decided, then she would do just that. After all, it was his own fault. He had made her give her word.

She clicked on the light beside the bed. "Mike, wake up, it's Sydney." Gingerly, she poked at the covers. *"Mike!"*

He shot straight up, and as he did, the sheet and comforter slid to his waist to reveal a broad and very bare chest covered with fine brown hair. "What the hell!"

"Mike, I've got to leave the island, and I can't wait until the one o'clock launch. What can I do?"

Mike's green eyes squinted against the light, then suddenly focused. "You're leaving?"

The covers beside him moved, and a sleepy voice from beneath asked, "What's going on?"

Absently he patted the mound. "Nothing, honey, go back to sleep. Now, Sydney, you can't leave—"

"I've *got* to!"

"Does Nick know? Have you told him?"

A head covered with tousled red curls inched slowly from beneath the covers, and blue eyes looked at Sydney with confusion. "Who are you?"

Sydney reached her hand across Mike. "I'm Sydney Delaney. How do you do?"

"I don't know." The young woman rubbed her

eyes, then looked at Mike, obviously thinking he might have the answer.

But Mike's attention was totally on Sydney. "Will you please wait in the other room so that I can get dressed? Then we can discuss this in a calm manner."

"I can't. I just don't have the time. But if you'll tell me how I can get off this island, I'll be on my way and leave you and . . ." She looked inquiringly at the very pretty redhead beside Mike.

"Leslie," the young woman supplied.

"I'll leave you and Leslie to get on with . . . whatever."

"I can't let you go, Sydney. You know that."

Leslie pulled herself up, patted several pillows into place, then leaned back against them. Only as an afterthought did she draw the sheet up so that it covered her naked breasts. "Did you happen to bring any coffee with you, Sydney?"

"No, I'm sorry."

"That's too bad."

"You might try room service."

"That's a good idea."

"Sydney"—desperation was edging into Mike's voice—"if you'll just wait until this evening, you can talk to Nick."

"It's an emergency, Mike, a family emergency, and I've got to go right this minute."

Leslie spoke up. "What's the problem? This is a resort, not a prison. Mike, doesn't the helicopter usually fly in to the mainland this time of day to pick up the mail?"

"Leslie, try to be quiet like a good girl."

"Last night you didn't want me to be quiet."

"I'm not believing this," Mike muttered to himself as his eyes searched the ceiling for inspiration.

"In fact . . ."

Sydney turned to go.

"Wait!" Mike called. "If you're going to use the helicopter, I have to give authorization."

"Then give it."

Leslie adjusted the sheet over her breasts. ". . . Last night I distinctly remember . . ."

Ignoring Leslie's seemingly perfect recall of their activity the night before, Mike said, "First tell me when you'll be back." But he was already reaching for the phone.

"I'm not sure."

"But you will be back, right?"

She threw him a surprised glance. "Of course. I haven't accomplished my goal yet."

Leslie broke off her reminiscing. "Hope everything works out okay, Sydney."

"Thanks, Leslie."

Sai was waiting for her in the hall, and if she hadn't known better, she would have sworn his normally expressionless eyes held laughter. "Sai, will you take me to the helicopter, please?"

He bowed.

Nicholas stood at the window of the control room, looking down at the casino. Behind his back, one hand was clenched and lay in the palm of his other hand. "Dammit, Mike, this is all your fault! You should never have let her go."

"I didn't have much choice, Nick. Besides, she said she'd be back. She will."

"But it's been three days!"

"She'll be back," Mike said soothingly. "In the meantime, we have other worries. I've received word that Mandarin has recovered from her infection and is gathering her forces." When Nicholas didn't say anything, he added, "And she's found out that Josh is dead."

A spasm of pain contorted Nicholas's face. "I would give all I possess if he were still alive."

"He betrayed you, Nick."

Nicholas shook his head as if in denial. Just then Julian lumbered into the control room and whispered something into Mike's ear.

With considerable relief on his face, Mike turned to his employer. "Sydney was on the evening launch, Nick. She's in her room now."

Nicholas wheeled away from the window. "Why wasn't I told?"

"You just were."

The first thing Sydney did when she got back to the room was take a long hot shower. The smells and the grime of the racetrack washed away easily enough, but the tiredness in her bones stayed. It had been a busy three days, she mused, but well worth the effort. Addie's problem had been solved.

Stepping out of the shower, Sydney reached for a towel. The friction of the terry cloth felt good against her flesh, stimulating the blood under her skin so that when she got through rubbing, her body looked pink instead of ivory.

She poured out a handful of lotion and began smoothing it over her leg, and as she did, her thoughts turned to Nicholas. Although she didn't like the lack of control over her thoughts, it was something she was beginning to accept out of necessity. For even in the middle of all the excitement in Melbourne, her mind would return to Nicholas. At night she would picture him pacing the length of his control room, or standing on the highest level of his suite above the casino, staring out at the night. During the day she would think of him in his house on the wild side of the island, and she would wonder if he slept.

And constantly her mind replayed their last meeting. He had said he wanted to free her from the chains of her stutter. That was impossible, of course. It couldn't be done. She knew that if she knew nothing else.

He didn't understand, and she couldn't explain. The pain went too deep. She could still remember those occasions when her family would visit other stations for socials and how embarrassed she would be when her stutter betrayed her and exposed her to ridicule from the other kids.

There had actually been a six-month period right after her mother had died when she hadn't spoken at all. But with a lot of love from her father and her sisters, she had gradually begun to speak again, acquiring the control over the words and her emotions that would later allow her to go out among people so successfully.

No, he didn't understand. But . . . "Dammit all!" she muttered as she realized that the most disturbing thing was that she wanted to see him again. Badly.

She slipped on her silk nightgown and stepped into the bedroom.

"Where have you been?"

Her hand went to her breast in alarm. "N-N-Nicholas! How long have you been here?"

"Long enough to decide that I would go into the bathroom and get you if you didn't come out soon."

She stiffened. As glad as she was to see him, she refused to let him put her on the defensive. "Nicholas, I am paying good money for this room, and as long as I am, it should be considered mine and I should be protected from intruders."

"And so you shall be . . . except from me. There is no protection from me, Sydney. Don't you know that by now?"

He was steps away from her, yet she could feel his strong will as if it were a black velvet lariat attempting to wrap around her and draw her to him. In defense, she reached for her robe.

"Where have you been?" he asked again.

"Didn't Mike tell you?"

"He told me that your leaving involved a family emergency."

"That's right."

"Why didn't you tell *me* you were leaving?"

No one had ever been able to get her so angry, so quickly. "Maybe, Nicholas, because you're so damned inaccessible!"

"My inaccessibility doesn't extend to you, Sydney, and I'll make sure Mike knows it." He reached out and, with a gentle touch to her throat, he defused her anger. "Why won't you tell me about your emergency?"

"I—I—I can't. It's a private matter."

He jammed his hands into his pockets. "Then tell me this. Will you be leaving again?"

"Not until I've won the five hundred thousand dollars."

"And of course you won't tell me why you want to win so much money either, will you?"

She shook her head.

"Rich or poor, Sydney, I've never begged anyone for anything in my life."

She found herself going to him and laying her hand on his chest. "I'd tell you if it involved only me, but it doesn't."

He glanced down at her hand. "I hope the man you're doing this for appreciates all the trouble you're going to. Is he a good lover?"

She whirled away, her anger leaping forward again. "Tell me you have no secrets, Nicholas! Convince me! Then maybe I'll tell you mine."

He smiled, but it wasn't a particularly warm smile. With an easy motion he grabbed the sash of her robe and pulled her back to him. "All right. How much have you won to date?"

"Almost thirty thousand dollars."

"That's a long way from five hundred thousand."

"I'll make it. I have to, and I have three more weeks."

"So . . . three weeks or five hundred thousand dollars, whichever comes first. That's not a lot of time, Sydney."

"You don't think I can do it, do you?"

"Very few people could. The point is, I don't care whether you do or not."

"Are you that rich?"

"Yes."

His simple statements always took her breath away. "What *do* you care about, Nicholas?"

"I care about a lot of things."

"But you just choose to let very few people know what those things are, right?"

"Correct."

"You protect yourself, Nicholas, so allow me my protection."

"I want you, Sydney, you must know that."

His words, spoken so matter-of-factly, scared up a thrill inside her. "Yes."

"Well?" His hand was on her throat again, softly caressing.

"I-i-it can't be," she said. "It just can't be."

"Why?"

"Because you want too much."

He gave her the gentlest smile she had ever seen, and it affected her way too much. "How do you know what I want?"

"You want everything."

"You're absolutely right."

His outrageous honesty was a hard weapon to combat, she thought wearily. "How can I fight you, Nicholas?"

"You don't," he whispered, and gathered her into his arms. "You don't." His lips grazed over hers. "I missed you, Sydney."

She felt something melt inside her and hoped it wasn't her strength giving away completely. Nevertheless, she admitted, "I missed you too."

Then her mouth opened hungrily under his. Emotions swelled—sweet needs and tempting desires. She wanted the aching sweetness that curled through her like ribboned fire, she wanted his tongue in her mouth, she wanted . . .

He slipped the robe from her shoulders and let it fall to the floor. With his lips he nibbled and kissed across her cheek and down her throat. With his fingers he pushed back her hair from her face, tucking it behind her ear so that he could kiss the sweetly scented pulse point there. He dipped his head, but suddenly stopped. "What is this?"

"What?" she asked, confused.

"Behind your ear. It looks like paint." He rubbed his finger across the place, then looked at it. "It's . . . shoe polish!"

"I—I—I must have missed that spot when I showered." Hastily she rearranged her hair so that it covered the telltale brown color.

"What in heaven's name is going on, Sydney? You disappear for three days, and when you reappear you have shoe polish behind your ear. Do you realize how much polish you would have to use before you could get it behind your ear?"

"W-w-well, I must have . . ."

"Don't even bother to tell me you were polishing shoes, because I don't think I would believe you."

She tried to summon indignation and failed. Neither could she think of an acceptable explanation. "What do you think I was doing with the shoe polish?" she asked very slowly.

"I don't know. Sydney, look at me."

Reluctantly she lifted her face.

"Are you in trouble?"

"No, of course not."

"Sydney, whatever's going on with you, I can help. Trust me."

Trust him? She had never even considered the thought. "Why should I?"

He smiled sadly. "I can't think of a reason in the world. Good night. Sleep well."

It was the early hours just before dawn, when night was fading and the day had not yet decided to appear. Sydney rolled over and thumped her pillow. Since two o'clock she had been trying to sleep, quite unsuccessfully.

She simply had too much on her mind, and she couldn't tune it out. It had been four days since she had returned from Melbourne, and the days had been full. She had been trying very hard to concentrate on her gambling and not let Nicholas intrude upon her thoughts, but she had increased her winnings by only twenty thousand dollars, so that now she had a total of fifty thousand dollars. At this point she should have had much more, and the fact that she didn't worried her.

She gave up trying to sleep and got out of bed. Her bedroom had a window that overlooked the back of the hotel, and she wandered to it. Leaning against the window frame, gazing out over the grounds, she decided that she was going to have to amend her plans and give up being so cautious. But to do that, she told herself, she was going to have to get her mind off Nicholas. He had the power to make her goal secondary, and she couldn't allow that to happen.

Yet each night Nicholas seemed to find a way to

convince her to spend a few hours with him, and she had to admit she put up very little protest. Although she was a long way from understanding him, she was growing more and more to enjoy being with him. Just last night they had sat and listened to music. It had been a pleasant relaxation for her, a break from the tensions of the casino.

Of course, the evening had presented a different type of tension altogether. Nicholas had stayed well apart from her, but he had touched her all evening—with his words, with his voice, and with his eyes. As usual, his presence had unsettled her, like nettles under the skin.

Outside in the pale light a movement caught her eyes. A man was making his way across the grounds of the hotel toward the thick vegetation that marked the beginning of the rain forest. She stiffened. It was Nicholas! Her eyes followed him, and a strange thrill coursed through her that for once she could watch him without his being aware of it.

He reached the edge of the landscaped grounds, and he was about to enter the forest when something stopped him. To her surprise, Nicholas knelt and carefully picked up a baby bird that had fallen from its nest.

He cradled it in his hand for a moment, and through the pale dawning light she saw his dark head bend to the bird as he stroked its feathers with one long finger. Even more astonishing, he appeared to talk to it. Then with extraordinary care he placed the tiny bird back in its nest. She expected that he would continue on his way, but he didn't.

Instead, he stepped back a few feet and waited. At first she wasn't sure what he was waiting for, but then she saw the mother bird fluttering above his head in a tree, and she realized he was waiting to see if the mother bird accepted the baby back in the nest.

High in her room, separated by distance and glass, Sydney sensed Nicholas holding his breath and, unaware, she did the same. The mother bird hovered above the nest for long moments, then at last settled into the nest beside her baby.

Sydney's gaze flew to Nicholas. A small, gentle smile slowly curved his lips as his eyes rested on the mother bird and her baby, then he set off through the rain forest.

There were two things that struck her at once. One, how alone he seemed as he walked back to his house on the wild side of the island, where he would sleep the day away until night came again. And the other, how gentle he had been with the fragile bird, how attuned he had been to what might happen. He had cared, and the mother bird had sensed it and trusted him.

Not for the first time, she told herself that Nicholas Charron bewildered her, and she wondered if such a man could ever be fully understood.

The lounge bar where Sydney sat nursing a tall glass of iced tea opened onto the swimming pool. The sun had already begun to set, and still Sydney didn't move. She realized it was the first sunset she had seen since she had been on the island. Usually at this time of day she was in her room, dressing for the evening ahead.

Clouds had been forming over the island all day long, and now the undersides were a brilliant red-gold. She wondered if there was a storm brewing. Certainly that might explain this vague aching of her head and the restless energy she was feeling that was making it impossible for her to relax.

Unexplainably she had been able to sleep after she had seen Nicholas in the hour just before dawn, so she wasn't particularly tired.

But there was something else bothering her, something that was niggling at the back of her mind and had been for some time. She had a feeling it was important, and she was sure it had something to do with Nicholas. If she could only remember.

The mention of the name Nicholas Charron had her jerking her attention back to the lady sitting beside her. "I'm sorry, Miriam. What were you saying?"

Miriam, an elegant middle-aged lady, was someone Sydney had struck up a casual acquaintance with over the past few days. Miriam's husband, an English banker, was an enthusiastic but not very skilled gambler. Miriam had told Sydney that the trip to the reef had been a tradeoff. In exchange for spending two weeks with her husband on the Isle of Charron, he in turn would accompany her to Paris for two weeks.

"I was simply asking if you had read that booklet of rules in your room, the one put out by order of Nicholas Charron."

"Yes, I have, as a matter of fact."

"Well, my dear, I don't know about you, but I resent being told that shell collecting is not allowed on his island. I've never heard of such a thing! This is a tropical island, after all, and a resort!"

Sydney had never met a person less in need of protection, yet she felt a strange urge to come to Nicholas's defense. "I think he's just concerned that the guests of the hotel not disturb the ecology of the reef, Miriam. In particular, I read, he doesn't want any of the giant tritons collected. They prey on the starfish that destroy the coral, and natural control of the starfish is far better than anything that man can do."

"Yes, the crown-of-thorns is a definite problem," Miriam admitted grudgingly. "And"—she leaned forward as if she were imparting a delicious bit of gossip—"I've heard that Mr. Charron is actually financing a study on the problem of the crown-of-thorns infestation of the entire reef. I'm sure he wouldn't want that information getting around. He's such a private man, you know."

"Yes, I've heard."

Miriam patted her gray hair. "I suppose, though, that all of his care is paying off. I went out in the glass-bottomed boat today. It was lovely and well worth the trip, although mostly what we saw was the staghorn coral. It was quite the most exquisite shade of deep blue. You should have seen it, my dear. And a school of parrot fish swam under us. From above they looked just like a blue and green cloud. Then we came upon a section of the tabular coral in beautiful yellows and pinks. But actually, you know, the really picture-book sea gardens can't be seen unless you dive down to them."

Sydney took a sip of her tea. "I understand the hotel offers gear and instructions. Why don't you try it?"

Miriam shuddered. "You couldn't get me into that water for an Oscar de la Renta gown. The Great Barrier Reef has the most poisonous snakes in the world, and then, of course, there are the sharks."

"Perhaps to get to the beauty you have to accept the danger." Now, why had she said that? Sydney wondered, and rubbed her forehead as her gaze drifted back to the setting sun.

Miriam shook her head. "You strike me as far too sensible a young lady to believe that."

"I used to think I was sensible too," Sydney murmured. And then she remembered what it was that had been bothering her. It had been something Nicholas had said before she had left for Melbourne, something about being at the lagoon at sunset. "Excuse me, Miriam. I've got to go."

She heard Miriam call after her, "Sydney, where on earth are you going? Aren't you going to dress for dinner?"

She heard, but didn't take the time to answer.

The evening quiet of the lagoon assailed her. The water, usually turquoise, had been shaded to amethyst by the evening light. Brilliant emerald ferns trailed down to the banks, and here and there wild orchids nestled. And in the center of all the beauty, the black swans of Charron sailed the bejeweled waters with confident serenity.

From a distance a bell rang. Three times it sounded, clear and true. And a remarkable thing happened. The swans began to stir. Breath lodged in Sydney's throat with anticipation, and her heart began to pound. One by one the swans raised their silver-tipped black wings and lifted into flight. A rush of wind from their wings fanned her face. They circled over her head once, then in glorious unison took off across the red-gold sky in the direction of the other side of the island.

She took deep, calming breaths, letting her body absorb the excitement of what had just happened. It was hard for her to believe, but at long last she had seen the black swans fly, and it had been every bit as wondrous as she had dreamed it would be. Their beauty and grace in flight had been a sight she would never forget.

But what about the bell? she asked herself. It was as if they had risen in flight in response to the bell. Could that be? And where had the swans flown?

She pondered what she had seen as she made her way back to the hotel. In the lobby she passed Sai. Just as he did every time he saw her, he bowed ceremoniously and moved silently on.

Miriam, on the arm of her Robert, waved. "There you are, dear. Do join us for dinner."

"Thanks, but I'm not hungry." Aware once again of that vague aching of her head, she gave a small laugh. "Actually, I've got a headache."

"But that's terrible! Go to your room and have a

nice lie-down. It's the very best thing, I find. I do it quite often, isn't that right, Robert?"

Her husband, a corpulent but pleasant man, nodded. "Quite right. Rest a bit, and then you'll be ready to give the casino a go." He rubbed his hands together. "I'm feeling lucky tonight, and I'm thinking of trying a spot of blackjack. I'm burnt out on roulette."

Miriam rolled her eyes. "I should hope so. Robert dropped five thousand dollars last night. That's at least two Diors."

Robert ignored Miriam. "Maybe some of your luck will rub off on me, Sydney. I've never seen such a player. You haven't won a fortune, but you're certainly working on it!"

Miriam tugged on his arm. "Come on, Robert. Can't you see that Sydney is dying to get up to her room? Try a cool cloth on your forehead, dear. Works wonders."

As Miriam began to lead him away, Robert raised his hand. "See you at the tables later on, Sydney."

Five

Once in her room, Sydney took Miriam's advice and lay down, but she couldn't get her mind off the swans. To have finally seen them fly had been an extraordinary experience. But as excited as she was, she knew that perhaps no one else would have been as deeply affected as she by the sight. Very few would understand.

She was tempted to pick up the phone and ring her sisters. They would understand, but she also knew exactly how they would react. Addie, with her otherworld ways, would say acceptingly, "Of course. I told you you'd see the black swans fly one day." And Manda, with her exuberance for life, would demand to know if she had followed the swans. But to follow the swans, Sydney first had to know where they had gone.

And she knew only one person who would know that.

In spite of the persistent throb in her head, Sydney rose and dressed in a strapless sundress made of a lightweight, clear gold silk. Without bothering about stockings, she slipped on a pair of golden brown high-heeled sandals. Hastily she pinned her hair up, then let herself out the door.

But when she reached the black stainless steel doors of the lift to Nicholas's quarters, she realized that she had no idea how to get the doors to open, since there wasn't a conventional button. Then she remembered that this was a *private* lift, and the two times she had been to Nicholas's suite, someone had taken her. The first time it had been Mike. The second time it had been Nicholas himself.

Now what? she wondered. In frustration she hit the wall with the palm of her hand.

"Tell me what that wall has done to you, Sydney, and I'll have it punished immediately!"

Sydney wheeled at Mike's voice. "O-o-ooh, thank goodness, Mike. I'm so glad to see you. H-h-how do I get up to Nicholas's suite? Is he there?"

Mike looked at her with concern. "Whoa, there. Slow down, sweetheart. Is there something wrong?"

She shook her head. "N-N-Nicholas. Is he up there? Can I see him?"

Mike fished in his pocket, brought out a key, and inserted it. The door opened. "Heaven wouldn't be enough to help me if I tried to stop you, honey. Go right on up."

Inside the lift Sydney leaned against the back wall and shut her eyes. She was being incredibly stupid, she told herself, running to Nicholas like this. But she had the urge to share with him the fact that she had actually seen the black swans fly. And she had a nebulous feeling that he had answers she needed. The problem was, she wasn't sure what the questions were.

"Sydney? What's wrong?"

Her eyes flew open to find Nicholas standing in the open doorway of the lift. Casually dressed in black slacks and a black silk shirt, and outlined by the dimly lit room behind him, he seemed to epitomize darkness, and she wondered if there was any light in him. Then she remembered the tenderness he had shown the baby bird.

"I—I—I just wanted to see you. Is that all right?"

"It absolutely is." He came to her and took her hand. "But you don't look well. Come, sit down."

She followed him to a level of the room she hadn't been to before, where there was a large lounging couch, extra deep and long. He waited until she was seated. "Now, let me get you something to drink."

She placed her hand on his arm. "No, please, stay."

Casting her a strange glance, he sat down beside her. "Sydney, are you all right?"

"I'm fine. I just want to talk to you."

"About what?"

"Nicholas, I saw the swans fly just a little while ago!"

He smiled gently, indulgently. "Is that what all this is about?"

"You told me I should go down to the lagoon at sunset, because you knew I'd see the swans fly, didn't you?"

"Yes."

"Why?"

"I thought you'd enjoy it."

"I did. But where were they going? And why?"

He stuck a cigarette between his teeth, lighted it, then sat back to regard her thoughtfully a moment. "They flew to the other side of the island."

"I know that," she said impatiently. "I could see. But where exactly and why?"

"There's another lagoon over there. They stay until dawn and then fly back. A couple of years ago one of the guests of the hotel became irate because he had lost rather heavily at the gaming tables that evening. He had too much to drink and wandered down to the lagoon, where he decided to take his anger out on the swans. He killed one."

She gasped in horror. "I don't understand. How could anyone kill something so beautiful?"

"Men don't always respect beauty, nor do they always respect life."

Absently she rubbed her temple. "I suppose that's true. And you're telling me that because of man's occasional disregard for beauty and life, the swans have to fly every evening to the other side of the island for safety."

He exhaled a stream of smoke so that it clouded the air between them. "That's right."

She gave a funny little laugh and rubbed her temple again. "It's odd, but when I was growing up on Killaroo, I never imagined that such wondrous creatures could be threatened by danger."

"Nothing on this earth is safe from danger, Sydney."

"I suppose not, but it seems that if there were any completely safe place to live on earth, it would be this beautiful island."

"Do you have a headache?"

She looked at him in surprise. "I've had one all day."

He ground his cigarette into an ashtray and held out his hands. "Come here."

Without thinking, she did as he asked, shifting closer to him.

He swiveled around on the sofa until he was leaning in the corner, and he pulled her back against him. "You're much too tense, Sydney. Don't worry about the swans' safety. They've found a place where they know they can be safe."

"I'm not worried about the swans. Really. I was just curious."

"So now you know. And there's no reason to worry about anything else either."

One by one he pulled the pins from her hair until it hung in a wild, glorious tumble around her head. It felt good, she admitted, to have the restriction of the tight pins gone.

"You have beautiful hair, Sydney. Why do you insist on wearing it up?"

Before she could answer, before she knew what he was going to do, he spread his fingers and began combing through her hair, again and again, until gradually she started to relax and her back curved naturally against his chest and her hands lay open on her lap.

Combing her hair with his fingers was an exquisitely intimate thing for him to do, she thought. And this from a man who had ordered his life to avoid intimacy.

"Nicholas?"

"Ummm?"

"The other night I asked you why you kept yourself apart from people. You never answered me."

"I know."

His voice came to her very softly, as if he were immersed in the way her hair felt as his fingers ran rhythmically through it. Her pain was vanishing, but still she lay against him, absorbing his heat. "You don't like anyone to get too close, do you?"

"You can get as close as you like."

It seemed to her that the temperature of his body suddenly went up. "W-w-why won't you answer my questions directly?"

His hands cupped her bare shoulders with a slight pressure. "Relax."

"Th-th-then tell me, why do you keep yourself apart from people and from life?"

He remained silent as he worked his fingertips in tiny circular motions up the sides of her neck, spiraling ever higher until his fingers were rotating across her scalp.

Finally he said, "The answer to that question is probably so complicated, I'm not even sure I know. Life takes a lot of twists and turns, and ten years ago mine took a major one. I lost my best friend, a man I loved more than a brother. And a woman I admired and respected has suffered undeservingly ever since."

Slowly his fingers circled the crown of her head. He reached her forehead, and there drew long, smoothing strokes from the center out to her hairline, where he ended up tracing small ovals on her temples.

She waited, wanting him to say more, but all he said was, "It's been a long ten years for me. Wounds close, Sydney, but sometimes the pain remains."

"I'm so sorry," she said, wanting immediately to comfort him.

"It's not your sympathy I want." All at once he shifted to the left and turned her around so that she faced him and was lying across his lap. She looked up at him and was entrapped by the way the candlelight played over the angles and planes of his dark face. "What I do want, though," he murmured, "is everything you're capable of giving and then more."

Why, oh, why did he have to say things like that? Sydney wondered with despair. Tonight he had told her a small bit about himself, allowing her to catch a glimpse of vulnerability in him. And he had soothed away her headache. All in all, he had managed to ignite in her all kinds of emotions, both physically and mentally, that she didn't know how to handle.

But he didn't even give her a chance to try. Over the golden silk of her dress, his hand cupped her breast, and heat flared in the pit of her stomach.

"If you'll let me, Sydney, I can reach inside you and touch all the places that will set you free."

Tension ebbed out of her as a soothing sensuality entered. She closed her eyes and listened to his voice, low and exciting.

With a slight pressure under her breast, he pushed so that the ivory-toned softness of her flesh mounded high above her strapless dress. "I like you in this dress," he whispered. "I like the way your breasts give the bodice its shape. And I like the way the neckline dips, giving me a glimpse of the shadowed valley between your breasts. . . ."

As he spoke, the thumbnail of his other hand traced up and down the line of her zipper. ". . . And I like this zipper, because it makes it so very simple for me to undress you . . ."

The sensual tingle of the zipper as it rasped against her skin mesmerized her so that for a moment she wasn't even aware that he had unzipped her dress. But then each of his fingertips stroked down her spine to her waist, and her dress slowly fell away from her.

". . . so that I can touch you just as I've wanted to, completely and unreservedly, ever since that first night I saw you. That night I wondered what velvet would taste like."

He bent his head, fastened his mouth over her nipple, and began to suckle. Potent emotions stirred and moved within her, and heat flowed through her veins so hot and thick she was afraid she might suffocate.

When at last he lifted his head, her eyes were drawn inexorably to his mouth. "Velvet tastes like rich sweet cream," he murmured.

His thumb grazed across the tight bud. A wash of intense pleasure flooded her, and in response she tightened her hands into fists as a means of reminding herself to retain some control. But he didn't let up.

". . . cream poured over fresh flowers."

A deep sigh escaped her mouth right before he claimed her lips in a searing kiss that soon had her arching against him in frantic need. His tongue in her mouth incited an urgency in her; his hands

America's most popular, most compelling romance novels...

Here, at last...love stories that really involve you!
Fresh, finely crafted novels with story lines so
believable you'll feel you're actually living them!
Characters you can relate to...exciting places to
visit...unexpected plot twists...all in all, exciting
romances that satisfy your mind and delight
your heart.

Now you can be sure you'll never, ever miss a single Loveswept title by enrolling in our special reader's home delivery service. A service that will bring all four new Loveswept romances published every month into your home—and deliver them to you before they appear in the bookstores!

Examine 4 Loveswept Novels for

15 days FREE!

(SEE OTHER SIDE FOR DETAILS)

on her skin created a fire. She was losing her fight for command over a steadily growing passion.

Over and over again he kissed her, until her hands had unfolded from their fists and were clinging to his shoulders. The muscles beneath the black silk of his shirt rippled and bunched as his hands smoothed over her skin, raising sensitivity and desire.

"Let go of that control of yours, Sydney, and let me show you how it can be between you and me."

He overwhelmed her with his power. He mystified her with his darkness. And, Lord help her, she thought, but she wanted him.

"You are so beautiful, so sweet. I want to taste you again," he whispered, arching her away from him so that his mouth could find her nipple once more.

Sensation flowed, resistance ebbed, desire threatened to take over. With his lips at her breast he was altering reality, and at the realization, a small cry left her mouth.

What was she thinking of? she asked herself. She was on the verge of giving herself completely to this exotic, mysterious man, of exceeding a boundary she herself had set. A new emotion assaulted her, and she recognized it instantly as fear.

She had gone almost to the edge with him. If she let him take her past that edge, what would be there waiting for her? She had no way of knowing, and that was what frightened her.

Her first instincts about him had been right. The man was danger personified. He was like his namesake, Charon, the dark, mystical figure in

Greek mythology who had power over men's souls, ferrying them to the other world across the River Styx. She had the distinct impression her soul could be in peril.

She pushed away and shakily pulled up her dress, covering her nakedness.

"What is it?" he asked, his voice a husky whisper that beckoned her back into his arms.

She rose and zipped her dress. "I—I—I can't go through with this, Nicholas. You're asking too much."

Although his chest showed the exertion of his trying to get his breathing under control, he studied her very calmly. With deliberate movement he reached for his cigarettes and lighter.

"Believe it or not, Sydney, I don't want you to do anything you don't want to do."

Her skin still felt the imprint of his hands. Her body still shook from the response to his lovemaking. She wanted him, and she was tired of fighting him. Still, she lashed out. "I—I—I find it hard to believe you're considering me."

He smiled faintly. "Perhaps you're right. Perhaps I am a selfish man. I don't know. I've never really thought about it before. But you see . . . sometimes when I'm with you, the possibility exists for me that night can be turned into day and the pain can be forgotten."

She stared at him in disbelief. "Th-th-that can't be true."

"It is. You have your own very special power, Sydney."

She shook her head in denial. "N-n-no. It's not true." Like steel to his magnet, she wanted desperately to go back into his arms. It was *he* who had the power. "I think I'd better leave now."

"Tomorrow night, Sydney. I'll see you again . . . tomorrow night."

She had no answer.

Sydney spent a sleepless night, tossing and turning. She knew that she could very well be about to fall into a trap from which there was no escape. With every encounter, Nicholas drew her closer and closer toward completely surrendering to a desire that would surely whirl her away into a world where there would be no control and very little light.

But there would be passion, she reminded herself over and over again until she was nearly writhing on the bed like a cat in heat. And there would be Nicholas. To some women, those two things alone would constitute an overabundance of riches. But she knew she needed more.

By morning she had decided. She had to leave the island. There was no alternative.

Hastily she dressed and packed. Then she reached for the phone and waited while she was connected to the opal field of Deadman's Ridge and her sister, Manda.

"Sydney? Why are you ringing so early? Is something wrong? Do you need Addie and me to come? Because if you do, I can contact Addie, no problem, and then Jacto and I . . . Sydney, why aren't you saying anything?"

"Probably because you haven't given me a chance," Sydney said dryly.

"Oh . . . well, then talk for goodness sake! Tell me what's wrong."

Sydney paused for a moment, mentally rehearsing what she would say. No matter what, Manda must not become worried about her. Manda had her own concerns, just as Addie did.

"There's no problem, Manda. I only rang to let you know that I'm leaving the Isle of Charron to go back to Brisbane. By this afternoon you'll be able to reach me at my flat."

"I don't understand. Why are you leaving? The last time we talked you said things were going well."

"They have been. In fact," she said, forcing brightness into her voice, "I've won fifty thousand dollars, but it's just not going as fast as I hoped. I think I'll have better luck somewhere else."

"Like where?"

Sydney had been dreading that question.

"*The Wombat.*"

"Isn't that the casino on the outskirts of Brisbane?"

"Yes."

"Sydney! That's an *illegal* casino!"

"I know, but it has definite advantages. It's in Brisbane, so I won't be out the cost of a hotel room, and I hear that the action is fast there. Do you realize all I would need is ten-to-one odds and I'd have all the money I'd need? If I can win the money ahead of our deadline, I would be free to help either you or Addie, whichever of you might need me the most."

Manda's answer was slow in coming, and when it did, Sydney heard the vague uneasiness in her sister's voice. "That would be great, all right, but . . . are you sure you're doing the right thing?"

"I'm sure. Now I've got to let you go. I'm already packed and about to walk out the door. Can you ring Addie for me?"

"Sure. But . . ."

"But what?"

"Didn't you say that you had some trouble getting off the island the last time?"

"Yes, but this time I know exactly where to go."

"Okay, then. Sydney . . . take care."

"Don't worry, Manda. I know what I'm doing. I'll talk to you soon."

Sydney hung up the phone and said a short prayer that she did indeed know what she was doing.

"Please hurry, Sai, open the door. I really need to talk to Mike."

Quietly Sai did as he was asked. This time, she didn't pause to look around the sitting room. She went straight to the bedroom.

"Mike, wake up. Mike!"

As before, he shot straight up. "What? Sydney? What?"

"I'm sorry to wake you, but I need to leave right away."

He groaned and rubbed his eyes. "Not again."

"Yes. All I need is authorization to catch a ride on the helicopter. So call whomever you have to, and I'll be on my way."

"Does Nicholas know?"

"He's sleeping. I don't want to wake him."

If Mike didn't catch the fact that she hadn't answered his question directly, it was because at that moment the mound of covers moved beside him and a muffled voice said, "Mike?"

His head swiveled toward the mound in surprise, and Sydney had the impression he had forgotten he wasn't alone in bed, although she didn't know why. It seemed he, like his employer, was used to a plenitude of willing young women in his bed.

"Go back to sleep, Kathy."

A blond head emerged and blue eyes gazed at Sydney accusingly. "Who's she?"

Feeling a sense of déjà vu, she reached her hand across Mike and said, "I'm Sydney Delaney. How do you do?"

"Mike!" Kathy wailed. "I don't go in for me-nag-eries! I told you that last night."

"I think you mean ménage à trois," Sydney corrected Kathy gently, barely able to keep from laughing.

Kathy looked at her blankly.

With a heavy sigh Mike reached for the phone. "I suppose it's another emergency."

"Yes." It was definitely an emergency, Sydney thought. "Thanks, Mike. Oh, and Kathy"—briefly she was tempted to tell Mike that she had liked Leslie a lot better than she did Kathy, but decided against it. Mike didn't need advice so much as he needed a traffic cop—"it was awfully nice meeting you."

It was good to be back in Brisbane, Sydney told herself firmly. Maybe it didn't have the glamorous ambience of the Isle of Charron, but this city that had begun as a convict settlement in 1824 had evolved into a pleasant place to work and to live and boasted its own charm, with streets named after ladies, such as Ann and Elizabeth, running parallel, and streets named after men, such as Edward and George, running crosswise.

Once at her small flat, though, she found that the place she had lived in for over six years didn't seem as comforting as she had thought it would. The furnishings and accents that she had so carefully chosen now seemed alien to her.

But this was normal! she reminded herself— getting up in the morning to go to a nine-to-five job, living on a strict budget, dating men who actually didn't mind the daylight. Damn!

She rested for most of the afternoon, or at least tried, but she was greatly relieved when the time came to dress for The Wombat. Aware that it would be quite different from the elegant casino on Nicholas's island, she dressed conservatively. At the last minute she added a thin silver chain from which hung a silver medallion. A cross was engraved into the silver, and in the middle of the cross, a turquoise stone was set.

The necklace was a family heirloom. When her mother had worn it, the necklace had consisted of three identical medallions that were connected. However, when her mother had died, leaving three little girls, ages seven, eight, and nine, bereft, their father had had the medallions separated, so that each child could have one.

"For luck," she muttered, and tucked the necklace inside her dress.

Six

The Wombat was crowded, noisy, and boisterous. Smoke hovered in the air, and scantily clad waitresses barely stuffed into their costumes kept the drinks flowing. Sydney supposed that the owners of The Wombat encouraged drinking to dull the wits of the people who came to gamble, with the expectation that it would increase the house odds.

Her respect for Nicholas suddenly climbed. He allowed no alcoholic beverages served on the floor of his casino. Although he had never said it, she felt instinctively that he wouldn't want anyone to lose money because their ability to think rationally had been affected by alcohol.

Now, where had that thought come from? she wondered, nearly missing a step. She didn't know for sure that that was his reason for keeping the bar separate from the casino. But with her next breath she corrected herself. Yes, she did know why. Nicholas was a man who cared about tiny birds. In his own way he would care about people.

With a disgusted curse a man vacated a chair and Sydney slipped onto it. The Wombat dealt four decks for blackjack, which was fine with her since that was what she had been playing on the Isle of Charron. This was going to be easier than she had thought, she assured herself, and as if to prove her right, she won consistently the first hour, quickly doubling her money. Her hopes soared. If she were playing recklessly, it was only because she wanted to win quickly. And it wasn't as if her tactics weren't working, she thought as she raked in another pile of chips.

Waiting for the dealer to deal the next hand, Sydney noticed the glass of champagne one of the waitresses had placed at her elbow sometime earlier. Since the heavy smoke had begun to bother her, she took a sip, welcoming the coolness as it slid down her throat.

"Why don't you let me order you a real drink?" the man next to her offered in a slurred voice that indicated he had had quite a few drinks. He held up his glass for her inspection. "Scotch is what you should have. Champagne is for wimps."

"Then I guess that's what I am. Besides, I'm not going to drink. I was just a little thirsty, that's all."

"You sure don't play like a wimp," he noted admiringly. "You can play right up there with the best of them."

"Thank you."

He leaned closer and she caught the full strength of his Scotch-laden breath. "My name's Harvey, by

the way, and you're a real beaut." He burped,
then continued. "I think you should come home
with me tonight."

"I appreciate the, uh, invitation, Harvey, but
no, thank you."

Sydney won the next hand and the next, and
her euphoria climbed. She hardly noticed when
she began to lose, because at first her losses were
minimal compared to her winnings. But soon she
was down forty thousand dollars, and she forced
herself to stop and take stock of the situation.
Sipping from the ever-full champagne glass, she
decided her losing streak was only temporary and
nodded at the dealer for the next card.

Thirty minutes later she was down sixty thousand dollars, and she decided that the temperature inside The Wombat must have climbed dramatically in that time. It was extremely hot. She
took another sip of the golden wine in her glass
and immediately felt a lot better. The heat must
be why she was having difficulty recalling which
cards had been played, she decided. Her usually
clear photographic memory was producing hazy
pictures.

Harvey patted her shoulder and fell against her.
"Now, don't worry, pretty lady. You're too good to
keep on losing. Your luck is bound to change."

"I hope so," she murmured, and righted him.

"Say, what's your name anyway?"

"Sydney."

Harvey gave the dealer a belligerent stare. "You
deal Sydney a good hand, or you'll have me to
contend with. She's going home with me tonight!"

Sometime later, Sydney studied her hand, trying

to ignore the dizziness in her head. She had been dealt a six and a four, and the dealer's upcard was a seven. The odds of her getting a ten or a card that counted ten were good, so she doubled down, doubling her bet, and hoping the one last card she'd get would give her twenty.

Sure that she could now begin to make up her losses, she waited for that card. When it came, she couldn't believe her eyes. A lousy *three*! The dealer turned up his second card—a duece—and dealt himself a jack. She groaned. She had thirteen and the dealer had nineteen. What rotten luck!

She took a sip of champagne. Automatically she reached for another pile of chips, but found nothing. Confused, she glanced down and discovered that she was completely out of chips. *She had lost everything!*

"How could you do that to her?" Harvey demanded of the stone-faced dealer. "Now she might not want to come home with me, and I've never seen anyone more beaut than her!"

"Sydney, thank goodness we found you!"

Sydney gazed down at her champagne glass and wondered how it could still be full. She had never once caught anyone filling it, but then, she had to admit that her attention had been on the game. She felt numb. How could she possibly have lost over a hundred thousand dollars?

"Sydney!"

That voice sounded exactly like Addie's, she thought vaguely, and wondered if anyone would mind if she lay her head on the green baize table for a minute or so.

Two hands grabbed her arm and twisted her

around. She blinked. It *was* Addie, and Manda was with her! She felt like crying. Her two sisters, always there when she needed them, had come to console her.

"If Addie hadn't been along, I would never have gotten through that crowd," Manda said. "Come on, we need to get out of here."

Sydney beamed at her two sisters. "I'm so happy to see you!"

"And we're happy to see *you*," Addie said, "but right now we need to leave."

She eyed Manda's shoulder-length cinnamon-colored hair curiously. "Have you done something different to your hair?"

"Possibly some of it is missing. I've been practically tearing it out by the roots on my way here, worrying about you."

Sydney frowned. "Worried?"

"Manda called a friend to check out this place and found out it was bad news," Addie said. "This place is raided on a regular basis. Now, come on, dammit, let's get the hell out of here!"

Used to such language from her sweet, delicate-looking red-headed sister, Sydney didn't budge. "I just lost everything," she told the two of them, tears rushing to her golden eyes. "I can't believe it, but he dealt me a three."

"Sydney's coming home with me," Harvey told Manda.

"Exactly who are you?" Manda asked.

"That's Harvey and he's drunk," Sydney explained.

"I don't think he's the only one," Addie murmured to Manda.

Sydney moaned. "Do you know what the odds are against me being dealt a three?"

"No," Manda snapped, "and at the moment, I couldn't care less. Now, come on. This place is creepy."

The risk of Sydney being whisked away before his very eyes spurred Harvey into action. He stood up, reached across the table, and grabbed the dealer's shirtfront. "You're gonna be awful sorry you dealt Sydney a three, 'cause she didn't want a three!" Then Harvey threw a punch.

At the same time, a bullhorn blared from the front of the casino. "All right, ladies and gentlemen, what we have here is a raid. If you'll just stay where you are . . ."

Bedlam broke out.

Manda pulled Sydney off her stool, and Harvey fell onto it, having just been punched in the face by the dealer.

"I'm going to be sick," Sydney announced.

Addie drew her close so that they were face-to-face. "No, you're not, do you hear me? You will not be sick. We are going to walk out of here, and you won't be sick. Okay?"

Sydney nodded.

Manda ducked as a chair flew past her head. Its trajectory carried it straight into the dealer's broad back, where it splintered into fifty pieces.

With Manda and Addie on either side of Sydney, the three of them began to walk toward the front exit. Fights were going on all around them. Dealers were grabbing their cash receipts in preparation for a hasty exit. The police were either involved in the fights or busy trying to break them up.

A roundhouse punch came so close to Sydney that she could feel the breeze. Manda scooped up a beer bottle and broke it over the offender's head.

"Take a big step," Addie instructed, and dazedly Sydney stepped over the body of a man currently down.

Harvey, in despair because Sydney was leaving, climbed up on one of the blackjack tables, grabbed a light fixture, and swung out over the crowd in dogged pursuit of his objective. Moments later, both Harvey and the light fixture came crashing down directly behind the three sisters.

Unaware of Harvey's plight, they kept walking. A big, burly man stepped into their path. Manda grabbed a full ice bucket and dumped it over the man's head. Surprised, he staggered back, and they walked on.

In front of them, a rather large policeman was carrying two waitresses, one under each arm like so much firewood, out the door.

Someone lurched into Sydney. She stuck her foot out to regain her balance and inadvertently tripped a man who was lunging for Addie.

Finally, at the door, they faced one last barrier—a policeman. "No one is allowed to leave," he said firmly. "Just go on back in. One of my men will get to you eventually."

Addie turned her dark brown eyes on him and smiled. "We're leaving now."

A disconcerted expression crossed his experience-worn face, and he nodded. "You're leaving now."

Addie sailed through the door, but when Manda and Sydney went to pass him, he stopped them. "No one is allowed to leave."

"We're with her," Manda said, pointing toward Addie, now standing outside.

The policeman looked at Addie and she nodded. "All right," he said.

"My car's over there," Sydney said, nodding vaguely toward the other side of the parking lot.

"You're riding with us."

"But you don't have a car in Brisbane," Sydney pointed out, smiling because she had figured that fact out.

Addie took the wind out of her sails. "We rented a car at the airport."

"And Jacto will drive your car back to your flat," Manda said.

Sydney jerked away from her sisters. "Jacto! Oh, I'm so happy Jacto came. Where is he? I've got to say hello."

A tall black-skinned man materialized out of the darkness.

"Jacto! How wonderful that you're here. I lost all my money . . . and . . . I'm going to be sick."

"It will pass and perhaps get better," Jacto said.

"I don't think so. Oh, help!"

"Take her over there behind that car," Manda told Addie, grabbing Sydney's purse from under her arm. "I'll find her car keys."

Addie held her sister patiently while Sydney's stomach disgorged the champagne. When she was through, Addie wiped her face with a handkerchief. "Now you feel much better, don't you?"

Sydney nodded obediently.

"Sydney! Sydney!"

Turning around, Sydney saw Harvey at the door

of The Wombat, being forcibly restrained by the policeman.

"Sydney," Harvey called, "I'll see you around sometime, okay?"

With an effort, she raised her hand. " 'Bye, Harvey."

Manda pulled the car to the curb in front of Sydney's apartment. "It's all right, love. Addie and I haven't reached our goals yet either."

"But I lost everything! I don't have one cent left."

"We have two weeks to go," Addie said in a soothing voice. "A lot can happen in two weeks."

"It's no use, Addie. Your magic isn't going to work this time. I'm worried."

Glancing in the rearview mirror, Manda turned off the ignition and pulled the key out. "Jacto's right behind us. Let's go in and see if we can't come up with some solution."

Addie touched Sydney's arm reassuringly. "That's right. After all, the three of us together are invincible!"

Sydney groaned. "Not when one of us has a hangover."

Nicholas, standing in the moonlit shadows of the porch watched as Sydney and two bright-haired women climbed out of a minicar. An Aborigine, having parked right behind them, soon joined them.

He heard one of the women, the one with the shoulder-length cinnamon-colored hair, laugh and say, "Jacto!"

The other woman had shorter hair, a flaming red. She said something that he couldn't quite make out, but he definitely heard a cuss word. It surprised him since she had such an angelic look about her.

But Sydney had the major portion of his attention. Her head was down, her eyes on the path. When she reached the steps, she looked back. "Manda, do you have the key?"

"Right here." Manda moved past Sydney and bounced up the steps, coming to a stop when she saw Nicholas.

Jacto immediately moved into a position where he could intervene if necessary.

Manda eyed Nicholas with interest. "Hel-lo! Who are *you*?"

"Nicholas Charron." He looked past Manda to Sydney, who at the sight of him had stumbled and fallen against Addie. "Are you all right?" he asked.

"She's fine," Addie assured him. "You're the one who owns the 'Glass Palace,' aren't you?"

"I own the Isle of Charron," he answered, and took the few steps necessary to bring him to Sydney's side.

Addie looked at Manda. "That's what I said."

Manda's eyes were on Nicholas. "Hi. I'm Manda and this is Addie. We're Sydney's sisters."

"How do you do," he said.

"Can we please go inside?" Sydney requested, not at all sure how much longer her legs were going to hold her up.

"Oh, right!" Manda suddenly sprang into action, inserting the key into the door and opening it.

As they all filed into the small flat, Sydney's head whirled, and this time it wasn't because of the champagne. What could Nicholas possibly be doing here? She had known that he might be upset to find that she had left, but she never for a moment considered that his anger would propel him off the island to find her.

Her eyes met his. Oh, yes, he was definitely angry, but he seemed to be dealing with another emotion too. How puzzling, she thought, and tried to decide what to do with him.

With her two sisters, the tall, silent Jacto, and Nicholas in it, her flat seemed full to overflowing. She supposed that, technically speaking, she was the hostess, but for the life of her she couldn't think what to do.

Addie took the matter out of her hands. "I think Sydney could do with coffee. Why don't we all go into the kitchen?"

"Good idea," Manda said with an enthusiasm that Sydney wished for.

But then again, Sydney mused, following her sisters into the kitchen and taking a chair at the small table that filled most of the space in the room, Manda didn't know Nicholas. She didn't understand how he could take a woman and tangle up all her emotions so that she didn't know what she was doing.

Sydney decided to warn Manda and Addie. "Nicholas comes out only at night. I'm sure he's a vampire."

Her sisters looked at her worriedly, then Addie

turned to Nicholas. "She's fine. She's just had a sip too much champagne."

They didn't understand, Sydney thought mournfully, and dropped her head into her hands.

"Looks like she's had more than a sip too much," Nicholas murmured, gazing at her with a worried frown on his face.

"Never you mind," Manda said, pushing him unceremoniously into the chair across from Sydney's. "She'll be right as rain as soon as we get a few cups of coffee and some protein into her. I'm going to make some sandwiches. Would you like one?"

"No, but I'll take a cup of coffee."

Addie already had the pot perking. "It'll be ready in a jiffy."

Manda poked her head into the refrigerator. "Sydney, you don't even have a stick of celery in here!"

"Ivebeenaway."

"What?"

Sydney raised her head out of her hands. "I've been away."

Addie cast her a disapproving glance. "That means you didn't have anything to eat before you went to The Wombat. What in the hell were you thinking about? No wonder you got drunk."

"I didn't get drunk," Sydney mumbled.

"You went to The Wombat!" Nicholas exclaimed. "That place is dangerous."

"It wasn't so bad," Sydney answered.

"Not until the police came," Manda put in, her head now in Sydney's pantry. "Look, you've got some cans of tuna here. If we could lay our hands on some bread, we'd be in business. Maybe one of your neighbors has some."

"All my neighbors will be asleep," Sydney said. "Better send Addie."

Addie nodded. "Right, then. I'll be back soon."

Silently Jacto followed her.

Nicholas frowned. "Who is that man?"

"He's my friend," Manda responded. "We go lots of places together."

"What are you doing here, Nicholas?" Sydney asked.

"I've come to take you back."

"Coffee's ready," Manda announced, placing a cup in front of both Sydney and Nicholas. "Drink," she ordered her sister, then sat down to watch that she did.

Nicholas looked down at his coffee cup. "Sydney, can I speak to you alone?"

Manda crossed her arms over her chest and fixed steady amber eyes on him. "No, you can't. Not until she's feeling better. I don't know what's going on between the two of you, but I can tell with one glance that a person would need to be feeling at the top of her form to deal with you."

"It's all right, Manda." Sydney reached across the table and patted her sister's hand. "Nicholas, I can't go back to the island."

"I'm not leaving here without you."

"What are you going to do when the sun comes up?" Manda asked with real interest.

Sydney took a sustaining drink of the coffee. The heat and strength of it hit her immediately. "I can't go back to the island, because tonight I lost all of my money."

"*All* of it?"

Addie breezed in, with Jacto behind her. "Hi, everybody, we're back. Sydney, your next door neighbor, Mr. Carson, is a love. He gave me a whole loaf of bread."

"Mr. Carson is one of the grouchiest neighbors I've ever had, Addie, and no one who lives around here has ever described him as a love."

Addie's brows drew together in bewilderment. "That's funny. Oh, well, who wants sandwiches?"

Manda hopped up from the table. "We all do, and I'll help you make them."

Without taking his eyes off Sydney, Nicholas leaned back in his chair and lit a cigarette. "I don't understand how you could have lost all your money. You're just too good."

"She was dealt a three," Addie explained.

"And then there was the champagne," Manda added.

"What?"

Sydney pushed back from the table and stood up. "Look, I really don't want to talk about this right now. I'm going to take a nice long shower."

"That's a good idea," Addie said. "You'll feel lots better when you're done."

"And while you're gone, we'll get to know Nicholas better," Manda said. "Nicholas, how do you like your tuna sandwiches?"

Sydney was perfectly sure that Nicholas never ate tuna sandwiches. However, that wasn't her concern, she decided as she slipped from the kitchen and made her way into her bedroom. Although Manda and Addie were a formidable twosome, Nicholas was well able to handle himself.

She stripped off her clothes and stepped into the shower. Leaning against the wall, she let the water beat down on her, hot and hard, massaging her tense muscles and clearing her head.

But soon she became aware of tears slipping silently down her face and an awful sickness that ached in her stomach, and neither had anything to do with the champagne she had drunk. She had let down her sisters by losing that money, and more important, she had let down her father. Without her portion of the money, there was no way they would be able to reclaim the land that would make Killaroo whole again.

For long minutes she let the water pour over her head until her hair was soaked and the color of dark burgundy. Slowly the last effects of the champagne cleared from her head, and she began to feel more like herself. She wasn't quite so ready to give up as she had been. But what could she possibly do in two weeks' time, she asked herself, to earn, gain, or win five hundred thousand dollars?

And last but not least there was Nicholas—sitting in her kitchen. He had come to take her back. He could have his pick of the women at his casino, but he had come to get *her*. She was amazed.

She shut off the water and stepped out to dry herself and dress. Ten minutes later she was back in the kitchen, wearing a pair of jeans and a plain cotton blouse.

Addie looked up. "There you are and looking more like yourself, I must say."

Manda handed her a cup of coffee.

"Thanks." She glanced at Nicholas and found

him watching her. She looked back at her sisters. "Listen, if you wouldn't mind, I think I had better speak with Nicholas alone."

Sydney could tell Addie and Manda were dying of curiosity, but to anyone who didn't know them, there would have been no clue.

Manda picked up her coffee cup. "Sure, no problem. We'll just wait in the other room."

When Manda, Addie, and Jacto had left the room, she turned to Nicholas.

"Sit down, Sydney. Have some coffee."

She took a sip, but remained standing. "Hadn't you better be getting back to your island, Nicholas? It will be getting light in four or five hours."

"As soon as you say you'll come with me, we'll be on our way."

"You have never listened to me, Nicholas. I lost all my money! I *can't* go back."

Smoke from his cigarette momentarily blocked her view of his face, but she heard the anger in his voice. "And of course gambling would be the only reason you would want to go back to the island."

She looked away. "I couldn't even afford the price of a room."

"And if I said you could stay with me?"

"I'd say no."

"And if I said you could have a room in the hotel without cost?"

"I'd say no."

He crushed the cigarette out with particular vengeance. "And if I offered you a job?"

"A job!"

"A job, with room and board thrown in."

"Doing what?"

"As a dealer." She opened her mouth to object, but he held up his hand. "Hear me out, Sydney. I've never seen anyone better with cards than you. I've watched you, and I've finally figured out that you have a photographic memory. When you lose, it's not because you make a mistake in the count of the cards. As a dealer, you could put that ability to use for me."

"But—"

"I said, hear me out. Now, I know you have this obsession about winning five hundred thousand dollars. If I don't understand it, I accept it. So, I will stake you with ten thousand dollars. If at the end of, say, three weeks you have not made your goal, you will come to work for me."

"I don't have three weeks. I only have about two weeks."

"Even better for me. You'll be working for me that much sooner."

Never before had her perfectly ordinary kitchen seemed charged with so much peril. Briefly she wondered how he did it. He was sitting perfectly still, but she could feel his energy coming at her in waves. In spite of it, or perhaps because of it, she met his gaze steadily. "And what if at the end of that time I can pay you back your ten thousand dollars?"

He seemed to hesitate. "Then your obligation to work for me will be ended."

Her heart was thudding heavily and there was nothing she could do about it. "Why are you willing to do this, Nicholas?"

"You have an obsession, Sydney—winning that

money. Well, I also have an obsession." He smiled. "I notice you're not asking what my obsession is."

"N-N-Nicholas—"

"What's your answer, Sydney? Will you accept the job?"

She combed her fingers through her still wet hair. "Ten thousand dollars. That's a lot of money."

"Don't worry about it. I figure I can't lose. You'll either pay me back or you'll come to work for me. And either way I'll have you on my island for at least two more weeks."

"Y-y-you understand that most of my time during the next two weeks will be taken up with gambling."

"Most of your time . . . not all." He paused. "So, Sydney, what is your answer?"

She told herself that she had no choice.

She told herself that she could handle two weeks on the same island as Nicholas.

She told herself, but she didn't believe it.

"I accept. And thank you very much."

Seven

Sydney awoke late that afternoon in the room she had left nearly thirty-three hours before. Nicholas had wanted to give her a larger room, but she had remained firm that she would have the same small room. She would pay him back the ten thousand dollars, she told herself, plus the cost of the room and board. To owe Nicholas Charron anything might prove too costly. The emotional interest alone could bankrupt her.

Yet she had come back with him.

And although it was true that he was giving her a second chance to win the money that she needed for her father—and for that chance alone she would have done almost anything—there was so much more involved in her decision to accept Nicholas's offer, and she knew it.

He waited beautifully. And he watched. And he seemed to know that deep inside her, emotions were churning and building.

He wasn't a cold man; he was just a guarded

man. She knew all about guarding. She had fought all her life to conquer her stutter. He, on the other hand, had spoken of death and suffering.

He was a man who walked the night, because daylight was too bright and memories were too harsh.

Surrendering to him would be to be wrapped in night. But there were stars at night, scintillatingly bright, she reminded herself. And some nights were so soft and sensual, they seemed made of velvet.

The gambling was going well, Sydney reflected as she made her way back to her room for a respite. Time was too short for caution now, and this evening she had played all out. Of course, the luck of the cards decreed that she lose a certain number of hands, but her mind was clear, her resolve strong, and she had no doubt she would win the money she needed.

She inserted the key into the door and started to push it open.

"So, you're back."

She turned to find Mike, but a different Mike from the one she had seen before. Gone was his easygoing smile. Gone was the twinkle in his green eyes that she had grown so used to. The man standing before her was rigid with fury, and menace was written in every line of his body.

"Mike, what's wrong?"

"You might well ask. What was it, Sydney—a power play—leaving the island to see if Nick would follow you? You knew he would."

"Mike, I'm sorry, but I have no idea what you're talking about."

"First of all, you lied to me. It wasn't like the first time you left. You never intended coming back, did you? When I inquired at the front desk, I found that you had checked out."

"I'm sorry. I admit I misled you, but it was important that I leave. I knew that you would wake up Nicholas if I told you I was leaving for good."

Her apology did nothing to appease him. "And that wouldn't have suited your purposes, would it? You had to lure him off the island."

Her brow pleated in bewilderment. "Lure? Mike, I had no idea Nicholas would come after me. You have to believe me. And I think you'd better tell me exactly why you're so angry."

Mike studied her closely for a moment, obviously trying to make up his mind about something. "Don't you know? Didn't he tell you?"

"Tell me what?"

"Sydney, Nick put himself in serious danger by going after you."

"D-d-danger! What are you talking about?"

"If he didn't tell you, then he's not going to appreciate my giving you the details. All I'll say is that he was warned not to leave the island. I can protect him as long as he stays here." His face twisted grimly. "When I found out that he had gone after you, I nearly had a heart attack."

"I had no idea."

"Okay, I believe you, and I suppose I owe you an apology. But, Sydney, don't leave the island again. It's imperative that Nick stay where I can protect him."

"Mike, I have no power over what Nicholas does or doesn't do."

Mike's hard green eyes swept over her. "Don't you?"

When some ten minutes later she opened the door of her bedroom to Nicholas, the shock of what Mike had told her was still plainly etched on her face.

Nicholas had only to take one look at her. "What's wrong? I was watching you earlier and you were winning."

"I did. It's not that. Nicholas, Mike says you put yourself in danger by leaving the island to bring me back."

His dark brows drew together. "Mike says far too much."

"But is it true?"

He sat down and crossed one elegantly clad leg over the other. "Perhaps. But Mike takes his job too seriously. He's protected me for so long, he forgets I can take care of myself."

She dropped to the edge of the bed so that she could be close to him. "Nicholas, what is this danger? Why are you supposed to stay on the island?"

He smiled. "It seems I'm always telling you not to worry. Not," he added dryly, "that it seems to do much good. But in this case, please believe there really *is* nothing to worry about."

She crossed her arms. "Once again, Nicholas, you're not answering my question."

He eyed her thoughtfully. "And is it important to you that I do?"

"Yes, very."

He lit a cigarette. "Very well. I will tell you a little story." He gazed at the burning tip of his cigarette for a moment. "Some years ago I was captain of my own ship and involved in smuggling valuable art out of China during a time when, due to the political climate of the country, art was being destroyed. I had a rival, a very beautiful, intelligent rival, named Mandarin. She was at least as good as I was, and although she managed to slip away with treasures I had set my heart on, I didn't mind too much. I respected her, and after all, there was plenty for everyone. We each were managing to accumulate large fortunes."

He blew a heavy stream of smoke into the air. "As the fates would have it, Mandarin fell in love with my second-in-command, Josh. Josh was also my best friend. We played on the streets of Chicago together, and we tramped through the jungles of Southeast Asia together. But somewhere along the line, something twisted inside of Josh and never righted. It happened slowly, before my eyes, and there wasn't a damn thing I could do about it . . . except be there for him.

"Then one bright, sunshine-filled day, a trap was set for Mandarin and for me. I was lucky enough to escape, but Mandarin was caught and put in prison behind the bamboo curtain. For ten years I've worked to get her out, and I've finally succeeded."

Sydney slowly let out the breath she hadn't been aware of holding. "That's an incredible story."

His mouth twisted. "It isn't just a story. It was my life."

"I know, and that makes it all the more incredible. But I still don't understand. Why are you in danger now?"

"Simple. Mandarin thinks I'm the one who betrayed her and set that trap. Mandarin has sworn vengeance against me. If she had my respect as a rival privateer, she certainly has my respect as an enemy. She'll be deadly."

"You didn't betray her, did you." It was said quietly, a statement.

His dark brown eyes shimmered with feeling as they rested on her. "Thank you. And no, I didn't. Josh did."

She gasped. "Your best friend!"

"And Mandarin's lover. But Mandarin never knew, and the lady hates well. And now she's discovered an additional reason for hating me. Besides thinking that I set that trap, she also thinks I killed Josh." His voice dropped to almost a whisper. "She doesn't know that I would rather have given my life than have something happen to him."

Nicholas's pain was great. He handled it well. He concealed it well. But Sydney heard, and she had to fight back the tears she wanted to cry for him. "What really happened?"

He ground out his cigarette. "I suppose no one will ever know for sure. The best information I can get is that the Chinese agents—the same people who promised Josh a great deal of money for the capture of Mandarin and me—killed him."

Sydney was stunned. And she knew that nothing she could possibly say would come close to being adequate.

He stood and pulled her up with him. "So now you know, Sydney. But that knowledge alters nothing between us. You're a woman capable of great compassion and sympathy, and your golden eyes are telling me that this is what you're feeling for me. But once again, I must tell you that I don't want your compassion or your sympathy."

With his hands on her arms and his body so close to hers, Sydney's blood began to stir. He was right. Instinctively she had wanted to take him in her arms and comfort him. But he was a man who wanted no comfort.

Instead, he wanted what she had given no man before. Her passion. And in spite of her doubts, excitement began to climb inside her.

Then his mouth covered hers with deep hunger, and the kiss felt so right to her. His hands claimed her; her arms went around him. Mind and body, she returned the kiss, her mind spinning, her body pulsing.

She was aware that every time he took her into his arms, she was able to retain less and less control over her clamoring emotions. And she was aware that she was on the brink of being taken over completely by a fire so hot that it couldn't help but consume her.

But what could she do?

Nicholas felt her yielding. If she had been any other woman, he would have taken her then. But this was Sydney. And suddenly he knew that if he could give her nothing else, he would give her honesty. He managed to pull away, but he couldn't manage to take his hands off her.

His voice came roughly to her. "Sydney, I'm not

sure I have the ability to love. I think I possessed that ability once, but I don't think I do anymore. I only know that with every day that passes, my need for you, my feeling for you, seems to wind tighter and tighter into me, becoming part of me, until I can't draw a breath without wanting you to be there by my side to share that breath. I want you, Sydney Delaney, but you must want me equally. You must come to me."

And then he left her, and Sydney stood in the middle of her room, feeling bereft and shaken.

The swans had seemed to call to her tonight, and Sydney had come. Standing atop the sunroof of Nicholas's Glass Palace three floors up, she had an unrestricted view of the island, the lagoon, and the swans.

Gazing around, she wondered why she had never come up here before. It was a wonderful place, with plants and lounge chairs, tables and umbrellas. There was even a telescope set up so that the guests could bring the distant wonders of the island closer to them.

Yet tonight she had the roof all to herself. For most people, she was sure, would be in their rooms dressing for the evening ahead.

Feeling the swans pulling at her, though, she had dressed early and in one of her favorite gowns. It was of a bittersweet red silk that oddly enough blended magnificently with her unusual hair and warmed the ivory tone of her skin. The bodice would remind most people of a pinafore, but that's where any resemblance to a little girl's dress ended. It was true that the neckline demurely grazed her collarbone, but the back plunged to her waist, and the straps of the same material and color went over her shoulders to crisscross twice down her bare back.

Her gaze was drawn back to the swans. She wanted to see them fly tonight, and she wanted to see where they went. Now they sailed majestically on a gleaming amethyst lagoon, but soon she knew they would take flight into the remarkable golden-pink sky above them.

Curiosity drew Sydney to the telescope. Through it the swans appeared so close it seemed she could touch them. She swung the telescope around, scanning the island, the rain forest, and beyond, to the wild side of the island.

But then she heard the bell. She lifted her head and listened as it rang . . . once . . . twice . . . three times. As before, the swans stirred, then lifted their wings to the soft evening air. Sydney's heart lodged in her throat as she followed their flight. Their graceful black bodies were outlined against the pink sky as they circled above her, then headed toward the other side of the island.

She lowered her head back to the telescope, intent on seeing exactly where the swans were headed. As she swept the scope back and forth, she could see nothing at first but a blur of vivid colors and green forest. Gradually, though, by keeping an eye on the birds and their path across the sky, she began to concentrate on one area. It became clearer. She could pick out details. Then she saw.

There, on a headland, jutting out over the untamed sea, a house stood, rising from the rocky promontory. She almost missed it, so naturally did it fit into its surroundings. She might even have missed the T-shaped post and the large bell hanging from it. But she could never have missed the man. He was standing on a wooden deck beside the bell, dressed in a tuxedo, his head thrown back, looking up at the sky.

The man was Nicholas.

And he had called the swans to him.

For a moment Sydney felt weak. She pulled away from the glass and rested her forehead against the metal body of the telescope.

Lord. He had rung the bell, and the swans, wild creatures that they were, had flown to him. And they did this every night!

He didn't cage them.

But he commanded them.

They trusted him.

She raised her head to gaze through the glass again. Just in time to see the swans settle onto a lagoon in front of Nicholas.

His gaze was pensive as he watched them. His hands were inserted into the pockets of the tuxedo's pants. Standing so still and alone, unaware that she watched, he nevertheless had the ability to make her ache with desire for him.

What could she do? she asked herself.

What could she do about a man so dark in spirit he kept himself apart from all but a very few people?

What could she do about a man so sensitive that for ten years he had bled inside for friends lost?

What could she do about a man so formidable and powerful that he required an island of his own and a strike force of men to surround him?

What could she do? *She could love him.*

She could love him for as hard and as long as he would allow. It would be a time in heaven, a time in hell.

And she was going to him.

She raced out of the hotel, the red silk of her gown flying around her. And as always, Sai seemed to be there when she wanted him.

"Sai, I need to get to the other side of the island. I need to go to Nicholas. Can you help me?"

As usual, his black eyes regarded her without expression. Yet this time, for the first time, he spoke. "Are you sure?"

"Yes. I'm completely sure."

Without another word he turned and led her toward a parking lot and a Jeep with a silver and gray canopy. "Take the path at the back of the hotel and follow it." He withdrew a set of keys and handed them to her. "Good journey, Sydney."

She realized that he was talking about more than the trip across the island. "Thank you."

It was not night yet, but the rain forest allowed very little light. As she drove, she remembered that Nicholas had walked along this very path just before dawn. She at least had the headlights of the Jeep. He hadn't even carried a flashlight. He must have eyes like a cat, she concluded. But then, he was very used to the dark.

There was a smell of dampness all around her.

Occasionally she would hear the sound of running water over the noise of the engine of the Jeep and knew she was close to a stream or a waterfall. Now and again the headlights would pick out cords of orchids twining through the trees, and she could hear the laughter of a kookaburra.

Then, ahead of her, through a wall of leaves, she saw light—not much really, just a lighter shade of darkness—and she knew she had nearly reached Nicholas.

She broke free of the rain forest to a pink sky producing its last glow. The lagoon now populated by the swans was almost directly in front of her. She circled it and pulled to a stop at the bottom of the path that led up to the house.

She turned the key and listened. On this side of the island the surf was louder. Waves rolled across miles of ocean, unbroken by a fringe of reef, stopping only when they crashed onto the beach below Nicholas's house. But as loud as the surf was, she could barely hear the waves over the pounding of her heart. To her ears the pounding of her heart sounded like thunder.

She got out and took in her surroundings—the lush lagoon, the swans. Then slowly she lifted her eyes to the deck . . . and to Nicholas.

His stance was no longer casual. His arms were leaning on the railing, his body was rigid, and he was staring down at her, those dark eyes of his intense. Then suddenly he wheeled to move quickly down the steps. And she went to meet him.

Surprisingly he stopped an arm's length away from her. Yet even from that distance she could feel the heat of his need for her, and she was reassured.

"Are you totally certain?" he asked.

"Yes." Her lips curved shyly. "But you're going to have to help me, Nicholas. I'm not sure . . . I'll be able to . . . completely let go."

He stepped to her and with a great gentleness cupped her face. "You'll have to, Sydney. You won't have any choice, because I won't let you give me anything less than everything you have, everything you are."

The trembling began. She had known it would be like this—the fear and the anticipation of the unknown. Giving herself to this dark, powerful man would be the biggest gamble of her life.

Then there was no more time for fear, for Nicholas scooped her into his arms and began walking toward his house.

She couldn't have said what his house was like. Later there would be time to find out. She was being carried in his arms and that was all she needed to know for now. It seemed to her, though, that they passed through several rooms, and then they were in the bedroom.

He set her on her feet, and she received the twin impressions of spaciousness and darkness, right before he placed a hard kiss on her lips.

"Stay here," he murmured. Her gaze followed him as he moved around the room, lighting tall white candles. Slowly the room filled with a golden illumination, and she could pick things out. A glass ceiling sloped above her. And in the middle of the room the bed rested on a high platform and was surrounded by white gauze mosquito netting.

She reached to begin unfastening the straps of her dress, but his voice stopped her. "I want to undress you."

So he came to her and began to do just that—slowly and with exquisite care, until the bodice of her dress fell to her waist.

"Here." Her hand went to the back of her waist. "The catch is here." She was nervous and it showed in the too quick movement and in the shakiness of her voice.

His hand clasped hers. "Shhh. I told you, I want to do it myself." His voice flowed over her like satin sliding over raw skin, soothing, yet enticing.

With a flick of his fingers the dress was unhooked and it slipped to the floor around her feet. Left standing in only her panties, she stepped out of her shoes and the dress with one motion.

"You are so beautiful." The words were uttered on one long breath. The back of his hand slid down her throat and across the creamy skin of her breast, and his eyes followed the path of his hand. "I will not bruise you," he murmured solemnly.

Whether he was talking about bruises to her skin or to her soul, she did not know. And it did not matter. For she was sure that however many bruises and scars she would receive from this relationship, it would be worth it.

Smiling, she reached for his tie and undid it. "Now it's my turn to tell you not to worry." His jacket fell to the floor to join her dress. The studs in his shirt came out next. But there she stopped, for in all the time she had spent with him, she had never seen his chest. Dark hair matted across it, and she touched her fingers to the springy texture with wonder. Her lips followed. And in his chest a growl rumbled.

He raised her face to his. "To teach you the art of love will require patience, Sydney, but I'm impatient. My wait for you has been interminable, and I can't promise you anything if you persist in doing things like that."

"But I want to touch you."

"And I want to touch you. Now."

Once again he lifted her off her feet, this time to carry her up the steps to the bed. He parted the filmy netting and lay her down, and her arms reached for him, but he said, "Wait."

Without haste he discarded his clothes. By candlelight his skin gleamed bronze.

"I want you," she whispered, and he heard.

He came down beside her, and then they were enclosed in a soft white haze of gauze, and through the gauze, glimmers of golden flames danced around them. It was all so perfect.

But when his mouth touched hers, she froze.

She had thought she was ready. She *knew* it was what she wanted. But the reality of lying nearly naked on the bed with Nicholas was too much too fast.

"It's all right," he whispered, stroking her hair until it lay like a pool of spilled wine around her head. "We're going to take this slow, and we'll stop anytime you say."

Her hand touched his face. "B-b-but I don't want to stop."

"All right then."

His breath touched her lips before his mouth did. Yet, when she felt pressure against her bottom lip, she realized it was his tongue running across the fleshy center. Her lips parted for his tongue just as his hand cupped her breast. She inhaled sharply, then felt the strength and warmth of his body press against the length of her side.

He knew how to touch. He knew how to kiss. He knew how to make her respond, and she did. When he would have pulled his mouth from hers, she brought him back with a hand around his neck.

As he supported himself on one elbow, his hand rested on her forehead and the fingertips of his other hand pressed into the softness of her breast. He soothed even as he aroused.

After a while his mouth left hers and traveled to the underside of her breast. Tantalizing kisses were placed with the greatest of care to the sensitive skin there. Every portion of her breasts were touched by his hand, then kissed. The kisses were soft as a brush of a butterfly's wings in contrast to the rhythmic pressure of his fingers that increased by infinitesimal degrees. Every portion of her breasts was covered, first one, then the other, except for that part she was beginning to crave for him to touch. Her nipples.

She thought he could do no more. She thought his mouth would have to close over her nipple. Now!

She was wrong.

He opened his mouth wider and raked his teeth across the soft mounds, back and forth, back and forth, until her upper body bowed off the bed.

"You're clenching your fists," he murmured against her skin.

Was she? She hadn't even been aware of it. But she felt him gently open her hand and then his fingers entwined with hers.

"There, you see?" he crooned. "There's nothing at all to clench your fist over. Not yet, at any rate."

"N-N-Nicholas . . ."

"Shhh. It's all right."

She had no idea what she had wanted to say, but she knew she hadn't intended to stutter. She would have to be more careful. She would have to think first before she spoke. But thinking was abandoned when his mouth briefly touched hers before returning to her breast.

His tongue licked at the nipple, playing with it, teasing it and her. And his fingers took the bud and rolled it back and forth. He did everything but take the tight peak into his mouth. The ache in her stomach built excruciatingly. If he would only lay his mouth over the nipple.

"N-N-Nicholas . . ." *Damn, she had stammered again! She had to be more careful.*

Finally, and at last, his mouth took the nipple, and she wanted to cry out with relief and pleasure, but this time she remained quiet.

"Talk to me, Sydney. Tell me what you want."

She wanted to talk to him, God knew. She wanted to give him everything. Yet, in spite of what she wanted, she stayed silent. After all, he had her emotions speeding along like a roller coaster, twisting and turning, exciting and alternately soothing. She didn't know where he was going to take her next.

By remaining silent, she could handle these turbulent emotions, she told herself. She could have the pleasure of the lovemaking and still retain her control. It would be better that way.

And Nicholas would never know, she told herself, *for certainly she was responding.*

"You're holding back," he murmured as his fingers tightened around her other nipple.

How did he know? she wondered even as she once again arched to his mouth.

His hand slid down her stomach to the band of her panties and beneath.

Oh, Lord, the feelings! So many, piling one on top of the other, so potent.

"Let go, Sydney. Trust me. Let go."

He would never know how badly she wanted to let go. She really did. But she didn't want to stutter anymore. Not with Nicholas, not the first time they made love.

"Talk to me," he whispered, whisking her panties off. Then his fingers delved lower, through the nest of curls, and lower, to the opening where heat pulsed. "Does this feel good?"

She arched. "Oh-oh-oh . . . yes!"

"Good, good. How about this?" He pressed his finger against the spot that seemed to need his touch the most, and she couldn't believe the feelings that sparked out from the single touch.

All she could do was sigh her words. "Oh-oh-oh, Lord, N-N-Nicholas!"

"And I know that this will feel good." His finger began to move in tiny circles.

"Ahhh . . ."

She writhed as the pleasure rose inside her, like a wave, forming and reforming, gaining power and momentum as it went, looking for a shore on which to spend itself.

Then his finger dipped inside her, and his teeth gently closed around a nipple. At the same time, she felt his other hand stroke her forehead. There was no help for her. She could only feel and listen.

"You're going to do it, Sydney. You're going to give yourself completely to me, and when that happens, a whole new world will open for you. And I'll be there, making you feel things you never thought possible, taking you places you never knew existed, doing things to you that you've only dreamed about."

Pressure here, a slide of his finger across there. A nibble into soft skin, a bite of sweetness, a kiss of urgent hunger. *She was losing her mind. She was losing control. And she didn't care.*

She didn't care, because she was on fire, and a force had taken over her body—passion in its purest and most unyielding form.

It was with relief that she felt Nicholas slide inside her. But the relief lasted only moments, because he began to thrust into her with long, powerful strokes. She clung and moved and cried out, but he didn't relent. He was the one with control now, urging her onward and upward, with ever-increasing pressure into her, until . . .

"Nicholas!"

. . . together they soared like the black swans.

Eight

"You were a virgin."

It hadn't been a question, so she didn't answer.

"I've never been given total innocence before. Open your eyes, Sydney, and tell me why you gave away your virginity for me."

His voice sounded troubled, and as soon as she opened her eyes she saw that he was frowning at her. And probably, she reflected, her answer would make his frown deepen.

"Because I love you, Nicholas."

"I told you that I can't—"

"—love." His response had been a swift and automatic defense of a heart long guarded, she thought sadly. "I know. But in my short experience of love, it doesn't seem to matter if the other person doesn't love you back. You still love them."

"Sydney . . ."

She laid her hand on his cheek. "I came to you, knowing exactly what I was doing. I loved you, I wanted you, I trusted you. And so far you've done nothing to abuse any of those feelings."

"And if I do?"

His voice had hardened, sending a shiver down her spine. She wanted back the man who had so patiently taught her the art of lovemaking and then afterward had held her in his arms, soothing away the trembles and the tears of release and joy. "I guess I'll have to deal with that if and when it happens. In the meantime, I'd very much like you to make love to me again."

Although he was already leaning over her, he made no move toward fulfilling her request.

"What's the matter, Nicholas? Have you taught me everything you know?"

Her question so innocently asked spurred him to action. Nicholas spent the night teaching her, and before the morning came, Sydney was teaching him.

Light was just beginning to appear through the sloped glass ceiling when he murmured, "You're tired." He reached over to the bedside table and pressed two buttons. Shades automatically rolled down the ceiling, and heavy curtains swung across the windows, sealing the light out and the darkness in. "Stay here and sleep with me."

She snuggled against him and felt his arms gather her closer. And she slept.

To Nicholas, though, sleep didn't come as easily. For long hours he lay awake, listening to the roar of the sea and asking himself hard-to-answer questions. He had been honest with Sydney. He had told her more than he had ever told anyone else, and he had confessed that he didn't think he was capable of love. Yet she had come to him anyway. And now she was curled against him, sleeping peacefully, trustingly. Why did that bother him? Why couldn't he sleep?

Why was he so troubled? Getting Sydney in his bed had been exactly what he had wanted. The previous hours had been extraordinary. He had never known such gratification, such elation. *Why wasn't it enough?*

Before Nicholas woke and before night fell again, Sydney left his arms and made her way back to the hotel. It was close to the time when the guests would be dressing for dinner, so she didn't feel too out of place in her red silk gown. But as luck would have it, Mike, Julian, and Sai were all on the terrace when she climbed the steps.

"Good evening, gentlemen."

Julian and Sai nodded. Mike grinned. "That's a beautiful gown, Sydney. I thought so yesterday evening when I saw you in it."

Sydney refused to rise to his teasing. "Thank you, but I'm going up to change now."

"Sydney, wait up." Mike rarr after her, his expression now serious.

She stopped. "What is it?"

"I just wanted to say again that I'm sorry. I had no right to light into you the way I did the other night." He combed his fingers through his hair. "I was upset with myself for letting Nicholas get off the island in the first place, but I had no right to take my anger out on you."

"You didn't know he left?"

"Not until after he had gone. Nicholas answers

to no one, not even me, but in this case his actions could have had fatal consequences for him."

So cold did she suddenly feel, it was as though ice were melting down her spine. "It's hard for me to believe that anyone would want to harm him."

"Nicholas has many enemies, Sydney. The man commands fear, hate, and respect in equal measures from people."

"But what about love?" she asked softly.

"He doesn't want love."

She pushed a strand of hair off her face. "I know. But it doesn't matter, does it? You love him, and so do I. I'll see you later."

In her room she laid out what she would wear that night. Then she took off the red silk gown and stepped into the shower. She felt marvelous, she reflected, as she let the hot steamy water pour over her, easing the soreness in certain areas of her body. She was well rested and looking forward to the night ahead and the hands of blackjack she would play.

When sometime later she entered her bedroom, she saw that the light on her phone was flashing, indicating that someone had rung while she had been in the shower. Her pulse leaped into double time as she thought of Nicholas. But when she called the desk for her message, she found it was from a man named Dennis Billet. The message was simple. Manda needed her, and Dennis would pick her up at the Brisbane airport tomorrow.

Sydney hung up the phone and sat down on the bed. She had never met Dennis, but she had heard Manda talk about him before. Questions buzzed in her head. Why hadn't Manda contacted her herself? Was Manda ill or hurt? Maybe it would be better if she left tonight, she thought, already rising to pack. But then she stopped herself. Dennis was Manda's friend. If Manda had been in serious trouble, he would have arranged to meet her sometime tonight.

She glanced at the clock. She had time to pack, dress, and then go down and play a few hands before Nicholas arrived.

She played for four straight hours, and although she lost quite a few hands, she won most of them. She was pleased, she told herself. Her earnings were mounting. She still had a long way to go, but she was confident that she would arrive at her goal in time to help her father, plus be able to pay Nicholas back. Last night hadn't changed that resolve. She wanted no debts between them.

Reluctantly she pushed away from the table. She would have liked to have played a few more hands, but she needed to see Nicholas. She couldn't leave the island without telling him she was going. Not this time.

She made her way up to his aerie, stopping occasionally to speak with people she had come to know. Weeks ago she would have laughed if someone had told her she would be able to move through Charron's Glass Palace with complete comfort and confidence. And she would have called insane any person who tried to tell her that she and the mysterious owner of the Isle of Charron would be lovers.

But she *was* his lover, she reminded herself,

and in a matter of moments she would see him again.

She found him on the couch in the sitting area, reading through a thick report. It was the same couch she had sat on that first night when he had sent for her. He rose when he saw her.

She discovered she couldn't prevent the shyness that manifested itself in her voice. "Hi. Am I interrupting you?"

He held out his arms and she went into them. "An interruption from you is entirely welcome."

She had never known being held in a man's arms could be so wonderful. She could feel his strength; she could sense his care and need for her. When she raised her head to look at him, wanting somehow to let him know how she felt, he kissed her. She answered his passion fully; gone was the time when she would ever hold anything back from this man.

"Why didn't you wake me before you left?" he asked, still holding her.

She reached up to wipe a smear of her lipstick off his lips. "I didn't have the heart. You were sleeping so peacefully, and you were smiling, as though you were having a beautiful dream."

"If I was, I'm sure I was dreaming of you."

As she gazed at him, her golden eyes grew suddenly solemn. "Last night was marvelous, Nicholas. Thank you."

Furrows appeared in his brow. "You have nothing to thank me for."

"Yes, I do. I haven't stuttered once tonight. I've even been able to speak quickly without thinking about it."

Slowly the lines in his face relaxed. "That's wonderful. Come sit down with me."

"Wait." She pulled out of his arms and clasped her hands together. She dreaded this. "There's something I've got to tell you. I'm afraid I'm going to have to leave the island again."

Every line of his body and face tensed, but his voice remained soft. "You're not leaving."

"I have to, and I want you to understand."

"Save your breath, Sydney. I'm not letting you off this island."

Her temper flared. "I'll leave if I have to swim."

He stared at her a moment, his dark eyes flashing his own temper, then he reached for his cigarettes. Only after he had lit one did he speak again. "Are you a good swimmer?"

His question defused her anger. "Would you please sit down? I'd like to try to explain."

"Are you about to tell me at last why you're going to such great lengths to win five hundred thousand dollars?"

She nodded. "I'll tell you everything."

"Then I'll sit down."

Her desire for him to understand and accept what she was about to tell him overrode any humor she might have otherwise seen in the situation. She waited until he was seated, but she remained standing.

He raised a dark brow. "Well? I suggest you start with the man for whom you are winning the money."

"That's easy. He's my father."

"Your father!"

"Just listen, Nicholas, please. My father is a

good, hardworking man. Years ago, due to reasons that aren't really important now, he had to sell a large portion of Killaroo land. Ever since, it's been an obsession with him to get it back. Just recently he was given the chance to buy it back for one million five hundred thousand dollars. Manda, Addie, and I made a pact to earn that money. The catch is we had only two months to do it in, and our time is nearly up."

He let out a long whistle. "I can see one of you earning a third, maybe . . . *maybe* even two of you. But the odds against all three of you doing it must be enormous. Sydney, I hate to say this to you, but it sounds close to impossible."

She smiled. "Impossible is a word we Delaney's don't acknowledge."

"Apparently." He shook his head in amazement and took another drag from his cigarette. Then he looked up at her. "Let me give you the money."

"No! Absolutely not. My sisters and I will do this ourselves or not at all."

His eyes narrowed against the smoke. "You feel that strongly about it?"

"Absolutely."

"Okay," he said slowly. "I understand. What I don't understand is why you have to leave."

"A few hours ago I received a message from an old friend of Manda's. The message said she needed me."

He stood up. "Then I'll go with you."

"No! First of all, Mike has made it very clear to me that you shouldn't leave the island."

"Mike works for me, Sydney."

"He's your friend and you should listen to him. Second of all, if you show up at Manda's with me, you might upset the balance of things."

He bent down to grind his cigarette out. "*Now* what are you talking about?"

"You don't know all that Manda's having to deal with. I don't know all of it myself. But this I know—we can't have a lot of people descending on her. We must avoid raising suspicion at all costs, for her sake and for Addie's. That's been the reason for all the secrecy."

He moved to her and grasped her upper arms in his hands. "I don't want you to leave, dammit!"

"I have to, but chances are I won't be gone long."

"Well, then," he muttered, "if you're determined to leave, you're going to spend the rest of the night with me."

And then he lowered his mouth to hers for a deep kiss that didn't end until sometime just before dawn.

The night was moonless. The hour was two hours after midnight. The only sound that could be heard over on the wild side of the island was the surf as it crashed onto the beach. Nicholas crouched beneath a pisonia tree, using for cover the natural cave the tree's low branches and leaves formed. He gave little thought to the gun he was carrying. To him it was a natural extension of his hand and arm. Ten years of a relatively civilized life hadn't changed that.

Nor did he give the inert body of the unconscious man who lay several feet away from him any thought. He had hit the man with just enough force to knock him out for about ten minutes, having decided that that was all the time he would need.

The other man, the one he was watching now, crept closer and closer to Nicholas's hiding place. He wouldn't knock this one unconscious. He wanted him totally alert and capable of answering questions. Nicholas's gaze followed the man. Without knowing it, the man was making it incredibly easy for Nicholas to take him down, and Nicholas mentally urged him on. The man had to walk just a few more steps. . . . *Now!*

Nicholas lunged at the man and knocked him to the ground. In less than a second Nicholas was crouched over the man, his gun digging into the man's throat.

"Where's Mandarin?" Nicholas might have been talking to one of the hotel's guests, so calmly and quietly did he speak.

"I—I'm not sure."

Nicholas pressed the gun deeper into the vulnerable hollow above the man's collarbone. "Think about it. I'm sure you'll remember."

Just then gunshots were heard in the distance. The man beneath Nicholas stiffened.

"Easy, easy," Nicholas crooned. "The way I see it, you've got a fifty-fifty chance that Mandarin and the rest of her men will win that little skirmish down the beach. In which case, you've got nothing to worry about." The deadly click of the gun being cocked suddenly sounded. "Or do you?"

"I . . . I . . . I . . . ." The man was choking.

Nicholas eased the pressure of the gun slightly. "Did you decide you'd like to tell me something?"

"Mandarin stayed on the yacht."

"How many men came ashore."

"Twelve, myself included."

"And you were supposed to kill me?"

"No! No. Our orders were *not* to kill you. We were supposed to kidnap you and take you to Mandarin."

"So that she could kill me herself—quite slowly, I'm sure. How very vengeful of the lady."

"Nick! Nick! Where are you?"

Nicholas eased the hammer of the gun back into place and stood up. "I'm over here, Mike."

Mike came running up the beach with Julian and Sai close behind him. "Thank God, you're all right!" Mike glanced at the two men on the ground. "Any problems?"

"None. How about on your end?"

"We're all fine. There were no casualties, though two of her men were wounded. We have them down the beach. I estimate about seven or eight men escaped in the two power boats they came in on."

"Get up," Nicholas ordered the man on the ground. "You're going back to your boss."

"You're going to let them go?" Mike asked.

"They're of no use to me. Mandarin won't negotiate for them. You know that. Besides, I want a message delivered and this gentleman is going to deliver it."

Within fifteen minutes the three other men had been loaded onto a boat. Julian was guarding the man Nicholas had questioned. Nicholas walked up to him. "Tell Mandarin if she wants a face-to-face meeting with me, to take the afternoon launch from the mainland in five days' time. She's to come alone."

"She'd be a fool to agree to that," the man said.

A thin smile narrowed Nicholas's lips. "You obviously don't know how badly she wants to kill me. Tell her I will reserve a suite for her. Tell her I look forward to seeing her again." He nodded to Julian. "Let him go."

A short time later Nicholas watched as the boat sped out to sea. Mike stood beside him, his feet apart, his hands shoved into his pockets. "Are you sure that's the right thing to do? Inviting Mandarin here?"

"I'm sure." Nicholas paused to light a cigarette. "We were lucky tonight, Mike. Someone could have been seriously hurt or even killed—one of the hotel's guests . . . or Sydney."

Mike looked appalled. "I hadn't thought about Sydney. I guess whatever took her away this morning was fortunate. Otherwise she would have been with you."

Without taking his eyes off the ink-black sea, Nicholas said in a flat, matter-of-fact monotone, "That's right. If she had been on the island, she would have been with me."

Sydney arrived back on the island late the next night. Mike was standing on the landing as the launch docked.

"Mike, what a nice surprise!"

He dropped a kiss on her cheek. "The mainland radioed that you were coming in."

"Where's Nicholas?"

"He's waiting for you at his house. He gave specific instructions that you were to come right away."

A thrill shot through Sydney. Actually she had harbored a secret hope that Nicholas would be waiting for her on the landing. She had been gone two days and had missed him terribly, and she had experienced a pang of disappointment when Mike met her instead of Nicholas. Now, though, Mike was telling her that Nicholas wanted to see her as much as she wanted to see him. "But what about my bag?"

"No problem. I'll see to it. I have a Jeep waiting for you."

She couldn't drive very fast through the rain forest, and the short trip seemed to her to take an interminable amount of time. But at last the Jeep broke free of the rain forest. The black swans were already settled onto the lagoon for the night, and the lights of Nicholas's house could be seen clearly.

Sydney raced up the steps and entered the main room. As always when she entered a room, her brain received what she saw as a complete picture, and the picture she received of this room was a beautiful one.

As usual with the things that surrounded Nicholas, there was a mystery and a darkness about the room, yet with a wondrously tranquil feeling. Leaf-patterned Thai silk wrapped the walls. Fifteenth-century Chinese celadon plates, along with rare antique jade pieces, added subdued color. Cream suede couches provided a lightness. And a huge square lilac onyx coffee table reigned supreme in the center of the room. On it, a gem-encrusted vase held sprays of white orchids.

An ancient copper tiger guarded one corner of the room; a tall gold and bronze elephant dating from 980 guarded another corner. A statue of a horseman aboard his steed done in the three-color glazed pottery that was so widely produced in the early Tang dynasty adorned the mantel. And other precious Oriental art was placed here and there around the room.

Nicholas might have smuggled art out of China, Sydney reflected, selling it to private collectors to earn his fortune, but this house was proof that he hadn't been able to part with all of it.

It took less than a second for the entire room to register in her brain. The absence of Nicholas was notable.

But just then he walked into the room. He was wearing a beige sport jacket over black raw silk pants and a matching shirt. She rushed over to him, intending to throw her arms around him. "Nicholas! I missed you—"

"So you came back."

His tone, the rigid stance of his body—something was wrong! Instinctively she stopped a few steps away from him. "Of course I came back. Did you think I wouldn't?"

He walked to a side table and poured himself a drink. That was odd, she reflected. Unless it was wine with dinner, she had never seen him drink.

He took a long swallow. "You're a hard lady to

predict, Sydney. I really didn't know. At any rate, I'd like you to turn right around and go back to wherever it was that you went."

"I don't understand," she said slowly.

"It's simple. It's over." From an inside pocket in his jacket he withdrew a check. "This is made out in your name and in the amount you require."

"I—I—I can't take that!"

Something like pain crossed his face, then was gone so quickly she was sure she imagined it.

"You would have won it anyway, Sydney. This simplifies matters, that's all."

"But we made love!"

"We had *sex*, Sydney. Do you imagine you're the first woman I've ever taken to bed?"

"No . . . no." She ran her fingers through her hair. None of this made any sense. The man standing so coolly before her was a totally different man from the one she had left two days before. Maybe it was her Delaney pride, or maybe it was her Delaney stubbornness, but something was making it hard for her to buy what Nicholas was trying to sell her.

He emptied the contents of the glass down his throat and poured himself more. "I was totally honest with you, Sydney. I made you no promises."

"And I asked for none."

"No, you didn't," he acknowledged. "We had a good time, but— "

"A good time?" Tears sprang into her eyes. She hastily blinked them away, but she couldn't prevent her voice from shaking. "That's all it meant to you? A good time?"

He turned away from her as if he no longer

wanted to look at her. Or as if he couldn't, she thought. Was it possible that he was trying to hide something?

"I'm sorry, Sydney."

His apology stunned her. "You once told me that you never apologized. What's happened to change that?"

"Nothing's changed. Just accept that maybe this one time I am sorry."

"No! I won't accept that! I won't accept any of this!" She went to him and forcibly turned him to face her. "Now tell me what has happened since I've been gone."

His lips moved, and he almost smiled. Certainly new emotion appeared in his eyes. "When did you get to be so strong, Sydney Delaney?"

"For most of my life I've had to be. It takes strength to control a stutter."

"And it takes a different kind of strength to let go of the domination of your emotions that has controlled that stutter for so many years," he murmured, looking down at her.

He was thinking of the night they had made love, and Sydney almost shouted with happiness. She was getting somewhere! "Nicholas," she pleaded softly, "please tell me the real reason you want me to leave the island." She put her arms around him and hugged him close. "I know there must be one. . . ."

Sydney froze. Beneath his sport jacket there was a hard bulge. A distinctive bulge. And although she had never felt one in just those circumstances, she knew without asking that Nicholas was wearing a gun. She pulled away and looked at him with a question in her eyes.

He expelled a long, weary breath. "Why did I think I could pull this off? I should have known. You've proved the exception to every woman I've ever known since the first time I laid eyes on you."

"Is that a compliment?" she asked, trying to instill lightness into her voice, although a distinct uneasiness was now running rampant through her system.

"Take it as a complaint." He grinned and lifted the lid of a mother-of-pearl cigarette box, took a cigarette, and lit it.

"Okay, now suppose you tell me what's happening here."

He made a slow circle of the room, his head bent, occasionally lifting the cigarette to his lips for a hard draw. Finally he stopped in front of her and gestured toward the couch. "Sit down."

"If you'll sit down with me."

Humor leaped into his dark eyes as he bent to grind out his cigarette. "All right, Sydney. You're about to get your way. You can relax."

"Good."

While she took a seat on the couch, Nicholas shrugged out of his jacket and his gun holster. Carefully he laid them on a table, then came to join her. Sydney waited for what he was about to say, her heart cold. Somehow she knew that she was about to hear that the man she loved was in some kind of terrible danger.

"While you were away, Mandarin's men made an assault on the island."

Her gaze quickly scanned him from head to foot. "Were you hurt? Was anyone?"

"Two of her men were wounded."

"But you?"

He smiled and put his arm around her, drawing her against him. "I'm fine, but the point is, Mandarin won't give up. Knowing this, I sent her a message asking her to come alone to the island for a talk."

"Nicholas, that's so dangerous!"

"Not any more so than waiting, not knowing when she'll hit again or where."

"Do you think she'll come?"

"Oh, yes. She'll be here. I expect her to arrive in four days' time. That's why I want you gone."

"I'm not going anywhere."

He lifted her face to his. "Listen to me, Sydney. I have no way of knowing what will happen once she gets here. I can control the situation, but only so far, and that's why I want you out of the line of fire."

"I'm not leaving you. Besides, we made a deal. I'm going to win that money, because I have no intention of working for you." She repeated, "I'm not leaving you, Nicholas."

It was hard to tell with a man such as Nicholas, but he appeared moved. His hand caressed her cheek softly. "Sydney . . . you understand I can promise you nothing, offer you nothing. There's a large chunk of my life left unresolved. And because of that, there will be danger, maybe even death. Until it's resolved, one way or the other, I won't be free to face the future. Maybe not even then."

"I understand. Now you understand. We Delaney women are tough. When we love, we love completely. Maybe I will leave you one day, but it won't be today. And it won't be tomorrow, or even the day after. It will be on that day when I'm convinced that you really do want me to leave, and that there's absolutely no chance that you will ever love me in return."

Her words hit him with a force that left him breathless and confused. She was giving her love without reservation, baring her soul without regrets. To him what she was doing was overwhelming. "Sydney . . ."

To her he sounded almost helpless. She placed her finger on his lips. "Shhh. Don't say anything more. Just make love to me. I've missed you more than I can say."

He took her into his arms because what she asked was exceedingly easy for him to do . . . and because he couldn't do anything else.

Nine

Nicholas raised up on an elbow and let his gaze roam possessively over the woman by his side. Sydney was asleep. Her hair was spread in a wild tangle over her pillow, spilling over onto his and appearing an even deeper plum red against the navy blue sheets. Her lashes fanned out over the ivory skin of her cheeks. Her lips, swollen from his kisses, were slightly parted.

Carefully he lowered the sheet from her body to reveal bare skin that still, after countless hours of intimate knowledge, reminded him of creamed velvet.

His gaze traveled to her breasts that softly rose and fell with her breathing. Her nipples, those delicate buds he so loved to suckle until she would cry out for him to stop torturing her and take her immediately, were relaxed. On impulse he bent his head to put his mouth over one. Gently he sucked until the nipple stood taut and firm. Sydney moaned, but didn't wake. He switched to the

other nipple, and with attention managed to bring
it to the same state of arousal.

In her sleep Sydney's hips moved and her head
turned to one side. Nicholas wished he could leave
her alone, but he couldn't. He had never been
addicted to anything in his life, but he had to
admit that Sydney was coming perilously close to
an addiction with him. It both bewildered and
worried him, since an addiction implied a com-
pulsive need for something or someone. And there
was no way he could get around the fact that
something inside of him felt right and complete
only when she was by his side. As now.

He smoothed his hand down her stomach, then
back up. Her breasts fascinated him. His hand
closed around one perfect mound and gently
squeezed, lifting the nipple back to his mouth.
Hot and sweet, gratification flowed back to him in
boundless proportions.

Her body fed him. Her body satisfied him. Sydney delighted him in ways he had never known
possible, and he was amazed by all of it. When he
was inside her, it was as if he had never made
love with another woman. He knew he had, he
just couldn't remember, because Sydney had a
way of obliterating all who had gone before her.
He had come to hate the hours she spent at the
blackjack table, even while he had to accept it.

But every night she came back to his house on
the wild side of the island, where she gave him
her complete attention. In his bed, under the stars
that shone through the glass roof, she became an
untamed wanton, and responded with the innate
passion he had seen in her from the beginning.
God, how he loved her that way!

Even asleep she had the power to arouse him. The suction of his mouth increased. Completely ready for her as he was, Nicholas grew frustrated and impatient.

Instinctively her hips raised again, and this time Nicholas slipped into her. As her tightness closed around him, he shuddered.

Sydney awoke as he came into her. His dark brown eyes were already heated with passion, and she smiled dreamily up at him. But the dreaminess soon vanished and her expression changed to ecstasy as he thrust deeply into her with an ever-increasing rhythm of his hips.

Soon the heels of her feet were digging into the backs of his upper thighs, and her arms were twining tightly around his neck. From head to toe she burned. She wanted desperately for him to put out the fire. She begged. She grew mad with her need. She cried out. She shouted. And only then did he do as she asked.

Charron's Glass Palace was booked to capacity. Excitement was at an all-time high. It seemed that five nights before, a couple of the guests had wandered outside for a breath of fresh air and had heard gunshots. Those two people had told two more people, and those two people had told . . . The story spread.

There was no official version of what had happened, of course, since the ever-elusive Nicholas Charron and his men remained silent. But the guests on the Isle of Charron didn't mind. The rumors and speculations that were flying fast and furious through the hotel and casino were enough to provide entertainment and dinner talk for years to come. Some guests had even refused to leave when their reservations were up. After all, they had no intention of missing the excitement. Perhaps in years to come there would be a certain cachet in being able to say that they had been on the Isle of Charron at this particular time.

And now a mysterious woman had come in on the afternoon launch. Fred, the bellboy, said she had been whisked up to a large suite without even registering. Someone thought he had heard the name Mandarin. Everyone waited.

Sydney rolled her shoulders, trying to ease the pain that stabbed between her shoulder blades. The pain was caused by too many long hours sitting at the blackjack table, but there was nothing she could do about it. Hour by hour her winnings accumulated. She now had over two hundred and fifty thousand dollars, and if her luck held, it would take only a few more nights of gambling to reach her goal. The big help had come when the table stakes had been lifted for her, by Nicholas's orders she was sure, although she had never asked him.

But the tension of what she was doing was beginning to tell on her, for she could never let her mental alertness drop for one moment, since thousands and thousands of dollars were lost or won on the turn of a single card. And she couldn't let herself think about just how much money was changing hands or how much five hundred thousand dollars really was. She had to keep the figures abstract.

But above and beyond the tensions related to winning an incredible amount of money, Sydney was worried about Nicholas's safety. She knew that Mandarin had come in on yesterday afternoon's launch and had been sequestered in her suite ever since. Nicholas had sent word to Mandarin that he would see her as soon as she was rested. But thus far, the only people who had seen the woman were the room service waiters and waitresses.

Sydney indicated to the dealer that she would like her earnings added to her account, then left the table. Even though she spent her nights at Nicholas's house, she still kept her small room. Heading for the lift that would take her to the second floor, where her room was located, she saw a beautiful Oriental woman walking in the same direction.

An emerald green silk cheongsam skimmed the woman's small and delicately boned body. Against the emerald green her skin appeared as pale and translucent as the petals of a water lily. Her hair, black and straight, was pulled back into a chignon and secured by two elaborately carved ivory combs placed on either side of her head. Her eyes were black, almond-shaped, and harder than any eyes Sydney had ever seen before.

She knew without being told that this was Mandarin.

In spite of all she had been through, Mandarin was still a beautiful woman, but to Sydney's eyes she appeared tired. Her exquisite face showed strain, and there were deep lines beside her mouth and under her eyes. Normally Sydney's heart would have gone out to her, but this was the woman who was going to try to kill the man she loved.

The doors of the lift opened, and both women stepped inside. The doors closed. It didn't take Sydney long to decide that she couldn't let this opportunity pass.

With a movement so fast even she was surprised, she punched the button that stopped the lift between the first and second floors. Immediately Mandarin's head snapped around and she went into an automatic defensive crouch.

Sydney held out her hand. "Please, I'm not going to hurt you."

"That I know." Mandarin remained in a crouch, her blood red fingernails in position to claw anyone who came too close. "Who are you and what do you want?"

"I'm Sydney Delaney, and I'd very much like to talk to you."

"I know no Sydney Delaney."

"I'm . . . a friend of Nicholas's."

Slowly Mandarin raised from her crouch, but her eyes remained wary and the stance of her body was alert. "So . . . a friend of Nicholas's."

Sydney clasped her hands together, not wanting to make any inadvertent move that might startle Mandarin. "I just want you to know that Nicholas could never have done any of the things you think he did."

"Why, Sydney Delaney? Why do you care what I think?"

"Because there's been enough pain. Surely you can agree with that."

"I can agree with nothing you say . . . because,

you see, you are a friend of Nicholas's, and I am his enemy."

"But don't you see? There's no reason for you to regard Nicholas as your enemy."

Nicholas walked swiftly up to Mike, who was standing in front of one of the lifts, conferring with Julian. "What's up, Mike? I got your message."

"A few minutes ago Julian saw Mandarin and Sydney enter this lift together. Now it's stopped between floors."

Nicholas's face went pale. "Do you think the mechanism malfunctioned?"

Mike shook his head. "I'm pretty sure someone inside the lift stopped it."

"Oh, my God. Let's go up to two and pry the door open. Then I can climb down on top of it."

"Wait"—Mike grabbed his arm—"I don't want you climbing into it. Mandarin will be waiting for you. You'd be too vulnerable. I'll do it."

Nicholas shrugged out of Mike's hold and began to walk toward the staircase. "I'm doing it, and if Mandarin so much as lays a hand on Sydney, I'll kill her."

Mandarin regarded Sydney with something like curiosity. "You love him, don't you?"

Sydney nodded.

"Tell me, does he love you?"

"No . . . he doesn't. But it doesn't matter."

"You're a brave woman, Sydney Delaney. It would take much courage to love such a man as Nicholas Charron. Perhaps even more courage than it takes to hate him."

"But you've hated Nicholas all these years for nothing! Please, believe me!"

"What I believe is that *you* believe the man you love. But you must understand—I am going to kill him. Resign yourself. Start your grieving now. He not only took ten years of my life, but he also was responsible for two deaths."

"Two?" Sydney shook her head bewildered. "No, no. That's not right. I know you think he killed Josh, but he didn't. And there was no other life taken."

"Sydney! Are you all right? I'm coming down to get you."

Sydney raised her face to the roof of the lift. "No! Stay where you are, Nicholas. I'm fine, and I'll be right up."

"Are you sure?"

"I'm sure. Just give me one more minute." She turned to look at Mandarin.

"Two lives, Sydney Delaney—my lover, Josh, and my unborn child, who died in my belly before he had a chance to be born. Soon you, too, will know part of that grief." A red-tipped finger punched the button that started the lift.

Shortly thereafter, the doors opened, and Nicholas immediately rushed in. With a brief glance at Mandarin, he put his hand on Sydney's arm. "Are you all right? What in the world happened?"

Mandarin's gaze went first to Mike. His total attention was trained on her. He had one foot inside the lift, his body positioned so that he could spring toward her at a moment's notice. Her gaze switched to Nicholas. "Your lover was trying to plead your cause with me, Nicholas. It was really rather sweet. But you should have told her that I can't be swayed on the subject of my hatred for you."

With his arm around Sydney, Nicholas looked at Mandarin. "I was on my way to see you. I think it's time that we talked."

She inclined her head in agreement.

"Mike, take Sydney up to my suite. I'll be there directly."

"Nicholas, be careful." The words escaped Sydney's lips before she could prevent it. He was probably already upset with her for trying to interfere.

Nicholas walked her out of the lift and lowered his head to give her a light, reassuring kiss. "Go with Mike," he whispered. "I'll see you in a little while."

But Mike made no move to escort Sydney to the private lift that would take them to Nicholas's suite. His eyes were still on Mandarin, and he held out an arm, preventing her from stepping out. "Mandarin, I'll have those combs in your hair, please. And hand them to me *carefully*, teeth side toward you, ivory side toward me."

A hard smile curved her lips, but she reached to her hair and began slowly to remove the combs. "Very good, Michael. But then, you always were an excellent man. I believe I once asked you to work for me, didn't I?"

"Yes, you did. Now hand me the combs, and with the greatest of care." When he had the combs in his hand, he held up the sharp points to show Nicholas. "Poison, I'm sure."

Nicholas nodded, then cut his eyes to Mandarin. "I believe we have some things to discuss." He held out his hand. "After you."

• • •

The next two hours were the longest of Sydney's life. Mike excused himself as soon as they'd entered the suite, and she knew without being told that he was going to stand in the hall outside Mandarin's rooms in case he heard anything that would indicate trouble. Mandarin had been right when she said that he was an excellent man.

Sydney was standing, gazing blindly out at the night, when the lift doors finally opened and Nicholas walked into the room. She ran down to him and threw herself in his arms.

"Thank God, you're all right!"

"Of course I'm all right. Did you doubt that I would be?"

She could hear the humor in his voice, and raised her head to gaze at him. He looked tired. "What happened?"

"It's over. It's all over. She's finally convinced that I didn't have that trap set for her and that I wasn't responsible for Josh's death."

"But she's hated you for so long. How did you manage to convince her?"

Nicholas led her to the sofa and they sat down. "I had evidence that confirmed in black and white that I was telling the truth. But even then, it took some time to prove to her that the evidence was real and not forged."

"But you did convince her?"

He rubbed his fingers over his eyes. "I did."

"And it's over?"

He laughed. "You're as hard to convince as Mandarin was."

She laid her head against his chest. "It's just that I've been so afraid."

He put his arm around her. "You should never have confronted Mandarin. That was a dangerous thing to do."

"I know." She rubbed her cheek against his shirt. "How did she take the fact that Josh is the one who betrayed her?"

"Hard," Nicholas said simply. "She's been through a great deal. She's over the illness she contracted, but she's still not completely recovered, either mentally or physically, from her ordeal in prison. I've invited her to stay on the island for a while and rest."

"Do you think she will?"

"I hope so."

Sydney remained silent, enjoying the steady beat of his heart against her ear.

"Do you plan to play anymore tonight?" he asked softly.

"No. I want to go back to your house and spend the night in your arms. Will you take me?"

Sydney felt as if her entire life had been condensed down to the two cards that lay in front of her. Everything rode on her next decision. All her senses were operating on a heightened plane, and her brain seemed to be functioning on several levels at once.

For instance, she was completely aware of how smooth and soft the silk of her gown felt against her skin. The gown was her favorite, the bittersweet red silk she had worn the first night she had gone to Nicholas. She considered it good luck, as she did the silver and turquoise medallion that rested between her breasts beneath the bodice of the dress.

And she knew to the dollar how much the pile of chips beside her represented, the pile having grown to staggering proportions during the evening.

And although she wasn't looking at him, she remembered her current dealer's face as clean-cut, honest, and impassive. As soon as the word got around as to what was happening at her table, the pit boss started changing dealers every twenty minutes in order to insure that her table always have a fresh, impartial dealer.

Julian had set up ropes around the table to keep at a distance the crowd that had steadily formed during the last few hours. Although the crowd was quiet, Sydney felt she could almost hear them breathing, so acute was the quiet.

She knew that Mike stood to one side, with Sai beside him.

And last but certainly not least, she knew that up in his control room, Nicholas paced. She could feel him, just as if he were standing beside her, touching her. And because of it, she felt torn. If she called for a card and won, what would happen between her and Nicholas? Their deal would be concluded. She could give him back his money, and there would be no more reason for her to stay on the island.

No! She couldn't let herself think about it. She brought her mind back to the action at the table. As usual, they were playing with four decks. Four decks meant two hundred and eight cards. Four decks meant sixteen aces, sixteen kings, sixteen queens, and so on.

During the evening the number of other players

at her table had dwindled to just two, the others having dropped out to watch her play. That meant that the three of them weren't going through the decks as fast as they would have if the table had been full. But they were still more than half-way through the shoe, and any hand now, the dealer would shuffle.

Sydney could remember every card that had been played. Her hand stood at seventeen. The odds were against her. She should probably stand pat.

She raised her head to look at the dealer. Perfectly trained, his face gave away nothing, but she knew that chances of him making twenty-one were good.

One more card. If she called for one more card, she could conceivably reach her goal—five hundred thousand dollars, plus the money she owed Nicholas, plus enough money to cover the taxes. *Or she could lose everything.*

Sydney took a deep breath, and from a distance she heard herself call for another card. The card was dealt. The player played out his hand—nineteen. She looked at it, but couldn't have said what it was. She saw herself reach out and turn over her bottom card. The dealer said *twenty-one*. And a roar from the crowd erupted.

Sydney felt cold, then hot, then cold again. She couldn't tear her eyes away from the three cards in front of her. Over and over she counted and they still came up to twenty-one. She had done it! She had actually done it!

Everyone was trying to talk to her at once. Sai and Julian were beaming. Someone she didn't know patted her arm. Mike hugged her.

Numbness had taken control of her body and wouldn't let go.

Then Nicholas was there, leading her through the crowd to his private lift. In his suite he poured her a brandy and held it to her lips until she drank. The brandy scalded down her throat, and feeling and sensations came flooding back.

"Well, you did it."

Sydney turned and looked at Nicholas, sitting on the couch beside her. "I did, didn't I?"

The amazed tone of her voice almost made Nicholas smile. Except . . . he was experiencing an odd uneasiness, and, as a result, he was distracted. What was going on? he wondered. Then suddenly it hit him—Sydney now had no more reason to stay on the island. "I knew you would make it. You're smart, beautiful, and good. How could you miss?"

"Easily." She took another sip and let the heated liquid slide down her throat.

He fought back a panicky feeling. Was it possible that he was going to lose her because he was incapable of loving? He cleared his throat, but the strange lump in his throat didn't go away. "What are you going to do now?"

She blinked. "Now?"

He had to touch her, so he stroked his fingers down her hair. "You've accomplished everything you set out to do. What now? Do you go back to your bank?"

There was humor here somewhere, he told himself. Or maybe it was irony. Women had come and gone in his life, and he had never given a damn. But a temptress with plum-colored hair and golden eyes had come into his life and now he didn't know if he could let her go.

Yet he knew that he couldn't hold her if she didn't want to stay. And he wasn't even sure if he could *ask* her to stay. Because, when all was said and done, what kind of life could he offer her? Living inside a glass palace on an island that he wasn't yet sure he was comfortable in leaving would not be for Sydney. Could he make her happy?

And then there was the matter of love. She deserved it. He wanted it. He squeezed his eyes shut in a private kind of anguish. *Was it remotely possible that he could give and accept love?*

Sydney leaned her head on his shoulder. "Before asking me to make another weighty decision, how about giving me a chance to savor my triumph?" she asked lightly.

"Sure. I was just curious."

"One thing I do know, though. The casinos of the world are safe from me. I will never, ever gamble again."

"Speaking for casino owners everywhere, thank you." He paused. "I have a suggestion for your immediate future."

She lifted her head. "Oh?"

He bent to nibble on her ear. "A celebration—a very private celebration for two over on the other side of the island at my house."

"Perfect," she murmured.

Ten

Dawn was just a few hours away. Arm in arm, Sydney and Nicholas climbed the steps. Once on the deck, Nicholas turned to her and took her into his arms. Was there a sense of desperation in the way his arms had reached for her, she wondered, or was that just her own desperation she was sensing? It was as if an icy wind had blown through her and reached to her soul. From that first evening when she had raced through the rain forest to go to Nicholas, she had known that this time might come. Now it had, but she wasn't even close to being prepared for it.

Within the circle of his arms, happiness and sadness warred in Sydney's heart. Her goal had been reached. Her part in saving Killaroo was done. Tomorrow she would call her sisters and see if either of them needed her help.

But tonight she would be with Nicholas. And if it was the last time, she wouldn't complain. Or at least she would try not to. Nicholas had never spoken a word of love to her, and she had not prodded him. With Nicholas she had gambled and lost. So she would take the happiness tonight would offer and worry about tomorrow when it came.

"You're very quiet," Nicholas murmured.

She lifted her face to him, and her hair tickled her shoulder blades. "It's been a long night. I guess I'm just winding down from all the excitement."

"I'd like to think the excitement is just beginning," he said, and was rewarded by her laughter. He dropped a light kiss on her lips. "Come on, let's go in."

A solitary porcelain lamp cast a wonderful radiance over the room, bathing Nicholas's art treasures in a warm glow. Her mind flashed a picture of the whole room.

But there was something wrong with the picture. Something was out of place.

Unerringly her gaze went to the darkened corner of the room, where the copper tiger was supposed to be. She could see the tiger. It was just that he had been shifted to the right so that he no longer stood directly in the corner.

All of this information was relayed to her brain in a matter of seconds. She heard Nicholas ask, "Would you like something to eat?"

Acting on instinct that she didn't fully understand, she threw her entire weight on Nicholas, catching him off balance, and falling with him to the floor, just as shots began to ring out.

Quickly Nicholas grabbed Sydney and rolled her behind the couch.

"Who is it?" Sydney whispered.

"I'm not sure," he answered, all the while cursing himself angrily. He was a man whose way of life had taught him to have a constant awareness of danger. Yet tonight, because he had been distracted, he hadn't seen what he should have seen. And because of it, Sydney was now in danger.

Suddenly the gunfire ceased, and a voice Sydney had never heard before called out. "What's the matter, Nick? Where's your hospitality? Come on out and introduce the pretty lady to your best friend."

Nicholas fought against the bile that rose like acid in his throat. It was Josh! *Josh!* And he was alive! Nicholas could hardly take it in, but the situation demanded that he do so, and fast. There was a time when he would have given anything he owned to see Josh alive, no matter the circumstances. But not now. Not with Sydney beside him and in danger.

Nicholas straightened until he was in a sitting position behind the couch, but he kept his hand on Sydney's shoulder, pressing her down. "Josh, throw down your gun and let's talk."

Another round of gunfire peppered the room. "Sure, Nick, whatever you say. Wasn't that always the case with us. You gave the orders and I followed."

"Come on, Josh. You know that wasn't how it was. We were friends."

"Except you were the captain, Nick. You were the one who gave the orders. You were the one the men looked up to and followed. You were the one who got the glory."

Nicholas's mind raced. If only he knew what kind of gun Josh had, he could calculate how many bullets were left. Unfortunately he had no way of knowing if the shots that had already been fired had been heard at the hotel. Chances were they hadn't been. He had to keep Josh talking until he could think of a way to divert him.

"Josh, you have no idea how glad I am that you're alive."

"Now, why don't I believe that? Over the years I've kept track of you, Nick, old friend, because I knew I'd be coming for you one of these days." A hollowness undermined his laughter. "You know you cost me a lot of money. When you escaped the trap that had been set for you, the people I had been dealing with cut the money that they were going to give me exactly in half."

Nicholas heard a shakiness in Josh's voice that hadn't been there a minute ago. "There was no reason to set Mandarin and me up for money, Josh. We were all making plenty of money."

"But it wasn't *mine*, damn you! I wanted money of my own! And the Chinese offered me more money than I had ever dreamed of. Even when they gave me only half, the money they deposited into my bank account every month was enough to buy me the best opium. But when Mandarin escaped, the money stopped coming." A thready sound underlined with desperation erupted from him. "No more money, no more dope. You can see it, can't you Nick? I've got to have the dope."

"Let me help you, Josh. I can—"

"*Help me!* That's rich. You won't even come out from behind that damned couch."

"I will if you put the gun down."

"No chance. Besides, we're about to have a visitor."

"What are you talking about?"

"Mandarin, of course. I left a note at the desk for her with instructions for your night manager to call her at this time and read it to her. The note says that I'm alive, at your house, and anxious to see her. What do you bet she'll come running?"

Nicholas silently cursed. "Don't you think that Mandarin has suffered enough, Josh?"

"*Suffered!* Try doing without dope when your system has had a steady supply for ten years. Then see if your concept of suffering doesn't change."

"You're ill—"

"Stand up, Nick. I promise I won't kill you until Mandarin gets here."

Sydney grabbed the sleeve of Nicholas's jacket and whispered, "Don't do it."

"Come on, Nick. I meant what I said. I won't shoot you, not until Mandarin gets here. I wouldn't deprive myself of the pleasure of seeing my two best friends together after all these years." With that, he went off into a peal of laughter.

Nicholas bent down so that he could speak into Sydney's ear. "I have to stand up. If I can see him, maybe I can think of some way to get that gun away from him."

"No!"

He kissed her temple. "Don't worry. I'll be all right. Stay put. Under no circumstances move."

Slowly Nicholas stood up, and as he did, Josh stepped out of the shadows. "Josh!" He couldn't help the exclamation at the sight of his friend, he was so shocked. Josh's physical condition had deteriorated severely since Nicholas had last seen him. Josh's frame was skeletal, and his eyes glowed hotly with a wildness that came from a deranged mind. His heart clenched with anguish as he remembered how Josh had once been.

Josh appeared amused at his reaction. "Time has been good to you, Nick. All of us should be so lucky. Right?"

"Josh, let me get you some help."

"Didn't you understand me? You *are* going to help me. When I kill you and Mandarin, the Chinese will start giving me the money again."

"Do you honestly think you can trust them?" As he talked, Nicholas moved slowly around to the front of the couch, careful not to startle Josh.

Josh followed Nicholas's movement with his gun, and when his hand began to tighten around the butt to the point that the gun began to waver dangerously, Nicholas stopped.

"They want you bad, Nick. You should be flattered at the amount of money they're willing to pay for you."

"Josh—" The sound of a Jeep had both men looking at the door. *Mandarin.* If only there were some way he could warn her.

Nicholas quickly gauged the short distance between the two of them, then dove forward onto the floor and began rolling very fast toward Josh. Josh fired wildly. Mandarin burst through the door just as Nicholas's body thudded against Josh's legs, knocking Josh backward. Following him down, Nicholas threw his body over Josh's and grabbed the gun.

"Don't hurt him!" Mandarin yelled.

Nicholas pushed the gun across the room. Josh fought, but his body was so wasted, he soon tired. Nicholas waited until he was sure Josh had stopped fighting, then stood up.

Curling his body into a tight ball, Josh began to cry.

Mandarin sank to the floor beside him. Her black hair, loose and long to her hips, fanned around her body as she bent and tried to take him into her arms, but he pushed her away.

"Don't touch me!"

Mandarin looked up at Nicholas with tears in her eyes. "Will he be all right?"

"I don't know. Maybe with the right help he will be."

Mandarin reached out to Josh again and gently stroked her fingers through his hair. "He will be. I know he will be."

Sydney stood and wrapped her arms around herself. The events of the last few minutes had left her shaking badly. Her gaze was locked on the scene in front of her. For the first time since she had known him, Nicholas's shoulders were slumped, as if they carried too much weight. And Mandarin sat beside the man she loved, chanting to herself and to Josh, "Everything will be all right. Everything will be all right," as if saying it would make it so.

Nicholas and Mandarin's sorrow and their love for Josh filled the room, and Sydney felt as if she had no place there. Quietly she walked over to Nicholas. "I think I'll go back to the hotel."

Nicholas felt as if his mind had been split in two. One half was on his past and the scene in front of him—Josh and Mandarin, the lost years, the pain. In the last half hour he had experienced more fear and vulnerability than he had in his entire life. And as a result, his emotions were frayed to the point that he was afraid they might come unraveled at any moment.

The other half of his mind was on Sydney. She was his present. *He needed her.* The alien thought sounded in his head with an ear-splitting intensity. Sydney could hold him together and make him whole. He wanted her by his side always. He wanted her to be his future; he wanted to be hers.

He had been right. With her, night could be turned into day and pain could be forgotten.

He loved her. But the words wouldn't come. They were too new to him . . . too awkward . . . He needed time to figure out how to say them.

He patted the hand she had placed on his arm. "Maybe that would be best. I have to make arrangements for Josh. You go on. I'll see you later."

Sydney nodded, but unable to leave him so abruptly, she raised up on her tiptoes and placed a gentle kiss on his cheek. "Good-bye, Nicholas."

More than the word good-bye, Nicholas heard the tone of her voice. So this was it then. There would be no time to figure out the words. Sydney was leaving him for good.

The noonday sun was directly overhead in a sky

so blue it almost hurt to look at it. Sydney sat by the bank of the turquoise lagoon and watched the black swans as they swam serenely among the rushes. She had come to say good-bye to them. Tonight they would be back on the wild side of the island with Nicholas. But she couldn't be. She had rung her sisters this morning, told them that her goal had been achieved, and made plans to meet them.

Small lorikeets wheeled through the trees above her head in colors of green, gold, blue, and red, attempting to charm her. But her heart was heavy. By late afternoon she would be on the launch, heading away from the tropical beauty of the Isle of Charron and the mysterious, exotic man who owned it. She would never return, but her heart would always be here.

She had learned much since she had been here, the most important thing being how powerful love could be. Mandarin had been to hell and back, yet she was still in love with the man who had sent her there. A few short weeks ago Sydney wouldn't have understood that type of love. Now she did. Because she felt the same type of love for Nicholas. Drawing her knees up, she lay her head on top of them.

"Sydney?"

She tensed, not believing what she was hearing.

"Sydney."

Slowly she raised her head to find the man she had just been thinking about standing beside her. She stared with disbelief. "Nicholas! What are you doing here? It's daylight. The sun is shining."

He dropped down beside her. "So it is."

"But you *never* come out when the sun is shining! Why now?"

"It's simple. I finally have a reason." He reached out and touched her hair. "You know, I think your hair is actually redder in the sunlight."

"Nicholas, why are you here?"

"Because of you. When you said good-bye back at the house, I knew you were going to leave, but I had to make arrangements for Josh. So I called Mike. I'm sorry, Sydney, but if you had tried to leave the island before I saw you, you wouldn't have been able to. I wanted to talk to you first."

Her heart thudded painfully. "Talk to me? But it's over, Nicholas."

"It's over?" His eyes held uncertainty. "You mean you've grown tired of me?"

She hastened to reassure him. "No. That's not what I mean at all! I mean, I didn't think that you would want me to stay. You've never said—"

"I know, I know." He looked at her, then took her face into his hands. "Sydney, I want to try to explain if I can. It all seems so complicated and yet it's really very simple. I saw you and wanted you with a suddenness that surprised even me. And because I've always been a man who gets what he wants, I never doubted the outcome. But I hadn't reckoned with you.

"You came to me and gave me your innocence. I had never been given innocence before, in any form. And you gave me your love without asking for anything in return. No one had ever come close to giving me such a gift and with no strings." Nicholas paused, struggling to express himself. He knew that his words were coming out stilted, but he had too much to lose if he stopped. "Inno-cence, love, and beauty—weapons difficult to fight against, even for a man such as I.

"You broke the chains of my darkness, and for the first time in over a decade, I've been able to step into the open and into the sunlight."

Tears of joy filled her eyes, but she was afraid to read too much into what he was saying. "It seems we each had our own chains," she murmured. "You broke the chains of my stammer."

He wiped an errant tear from her cheek and smiled tenderly. "Only for you, Sydney, would I have been tempted into the sunlight. And it took a jolt to make me see the truth. I realized I was going to lose you, and I panicked. My distraction could have gotten us killed, except for your quick thinking. You saved my life, and in the East they say that if you save a life, that life is yours. I love you, Sydney. My life is yours."

Sydney wasn't sure her heart would be able to hold all the happiness she was feeling. "I'd rather *share* your life, Nicholas, and I want you to share mine. We have the world before us, and we have each other. I want to take you to Killaroo so that you can learn to love it as much as I do. And I want you to meet my father so you'll understand why Manda, Addie, and I were willing to risk so much in order for him to fulfill his heart's desire and reclaim the Killaroo land he had lost. Which reminds me, tomorrow let's go to Melbourne and cheer Addie on."

"That's fine with me." Gently he lowered her to the ground and followed her down. "But tonight I want you exclusively to myself, in my bed, under the stars, on the wild side of the island."

She laughed happily and wrapped her arms around his neck. "You'll always have me, Nicholas."

"I need you, Sydney," he whispered. "I love you. Marry me, and together we'll spend the rest of our lives in the sunlight."

Epilogue

Killara at sunset—there was no place in the world she would rather be, Cara Delaney mused as she stood on the roof of the keep of the homestead and gazed across the valley to the far distant mountains. The sunset had turned the wide sky above the valley into a living painting of brilliant colors: crimson and gold, magenta and vermilion. As always, the scene took Cara's breath away, and she never tired of watching it.

A wind swept across the valley and picked up the hem of her topaz silk dinner dress. The skirt, made up of yards and yards of tiny pleats, lifted and billowed in the air, the topaz color shimmering like the rays of the sun.

In utter joy Cara raised her arms and began to swirl and dance around the keep, breathing in the crystal-clear air.

To the man watching, she was the epitome of beauty—a whirl of silver hair, topaz silk, and golden limbs. She twirled and she twirled, right into the arms of her husband.

"I knew I would find you up here," Burke murmured, closing his arms possessively around her.

Flushed and breathless, she laughed. "And I knew you would come and find me."

"Of course. I always will."

Cara twined her silken arms around her husband's neck and threw back her head. "Oh, Burke, before I met you I never knew there could be such happiness." Suddenly she danced out of his arms. "Burke! Let's go for a ride before dinner. Please?"

Burke smiled his consent. *Quicksilver*. Cara would always be his quicksilver girl.

The hooves of the two powerful Arabians, Shalimar and Sheikh, thundered over the ground as Cara and Burke raced across the valley toward the setting sun. They had chased the setting sun together countless times, yet it was always new and exhilarating to them.

The sun continued its descent, the colors in the sky above them changed, and after a time they reined in the Arabians to a walk.

"I heard from Cougar today," Burke said.

Cara grinned. "And I heard from Bridget. They just refuse to take their retirement seriously, don't they?"

"You're right about that. Cougar was calling about a new security system he's devised, in his *spare time*, he said."

"Bridget was calling to check up on Mrs. Copeland. She said, 'Ach! That Esther Copeland is a good enough housekeeper, I suppose, but I just know that she could do with a little supervision every so often, now, don't I?' "

Burke's green eyes sparkled with laughter and matched the brilliance of the Delaney emerald he wore on his hand. "Do you suppose the two of them are worried that we'll find out that we can do without them?"

"That's exactly what I think. Let's invite them for a visit next week. I just love to see the two of them together. They're so sweet."

"I'm sure they'd be mortified to hear you say so."

"Well, they are. I love the way Bridget fusses over Cougar, catering to his every whim. And the way he can make her blush just by looking at her is marvelous."

"I agree."

"Oh, I forgot something!" Cara reached for her husband's hand, and they both drew their horses to a standstill. "I've got some news I've been saving to tell you."

Hope leaped into Burke's dark green eyes, and a tender smile curved Cara's lips. "No, I'm not pregnant yet. But I know I will be soon. I can feel it. This time next year I'm willing to bet that we'll have a baby in the nursery of Killara."

Burke reached for her, lifted her off Shalimar, and settled her across his lap, braced between the pommel and his stomach, as if she were riding sidesaddle. "I can't stand it when you're so far away from me."

"Neither can I." She rested her head against his shoulder as Burke reined Sheikh around and headed him back to Killara. Shalimar followed. "Burke, you do want a baby, don't you?"

"Why would you doubt it?" He sounded amazed.

"I guess because you never talk about it."

"That's because I've been very conscious about not tying you down, Cara. If I had my way, I'd probably lock you in the keep so that I could have you all to myself, but before we were married, you were accustomed to an extraordinary amount of freedom."

She gazed up at him, wanting to see his face. "Freedom is loving you, Burke. Don't you know that by now? I freely chose to love you and I've never regretted it for a moment. I'm only truly happy when I'm with you, and a baby would only add more joy to our lives."

"Oh, Cara, I love you so much more than I ever thought possible." His lips closed on hers for a gentle kiss. Cara sighed and twisted to get closer to Burke. The kiss continued and deepened as under the wide, darkening sky they headed home.

Later, at the dinner table, Burke said, "You never did tell me your news."

Cara dropped her fork in astonishment. "I can't believe that I didn't tell you! And this news is important too! You shouldn't sidetrack me like that!"

Somehow Burke managed to look innocent. "All I did was kiss you."

Cara tried to frown, but didn't quite pull it off. "Never mind."

"Well? What's the news?"

"Maggie called today from Shamrock with the most fantastic story about three sisters. You're going to be amazed when you hear." Cara's face lighted with a sudden thought. "Burke, I have an idea!"

"You can have anything you want, but let's wait until tomorrow," Burke murmured.

"Burke, let's go to Australia. . . ."

What's it like to have Pazazz?
Ask the Delaney Sisters.

Matilda
The Adventuress
Sheer Cinnamon

Sydney
The Temptress
Sheer Plum

Adelaide
The Enchantress
Sheer Fire

SHEER FIRE, SHEER CINNAMON, SHEER PLUM—three of eight dazzling Sheer Color Wash shades. All beautifully translucent, all wash out in 3-4 shampoos.

PAZAZZ® SHEER COLOR WASH.

Try them all and be Loveswept®

Pazazz Sheer Color Wash is only available in the United States.

© 1984–1987 Clairol Inc.